Frankencat
by

Kathi Daley

I want to thank the very talented Jessica Fischer for the cover art.

I so appreciate Bruce Curran, who is always ready and willing to answer my cyber questions, and Peggy Hyndman for helping sleuth out those pesky typos.

A special thank you to Darla Taylor, Vivian Shane, Marie Rice, and Patty Liu for submitting recipes.

And, of course, thanks to the readers and bloggers in my life, who make doing what I do possible.

Thank you to Randy Ladenheim-Gil for the editing.

And finally I want to thank my sister Christy for always lending an ear and my husband Ken for allowing me time to write by taking care of everything else.

Books by Kathi Daley

Come for the murder, stay for the romance.

Zoe Donovan Cozy Mystery:
Halloween Hijinks
The Trouble With Turkeys
Christmas Crazy
Cupid's Curse
Big Bunny Bump-off
Beach Blanket Barbie
Maui Madness
Derby Divas
Haunted Hamlet
Turkeys, Tuxes, and Tabbies
Christmas Cozy
Alaskan Alliance
Matrimony Meltdown
Soul Surrender
Heavenly Honeymoon
Hopscotch Homicide
Ghostly Graveyard
Santa Sleuth
Shamrock Shenanigans
Kitten Kaboodle
Costume Catastrophe
Candy Cane Caper
Holiday Hangover
Easter Escapade
Camp Carter
Trick or Treason – *September 2017*
Reindeer Roundup – *December 2017*

Zimmerman Academy The New Normal
Ashton Falls Cozy Cookbook

Tj Jensen Paradise Lake Mysteries by Henery Press:
Pumpkins in Paradise
Snowmen in Paradise
Bikinis in Paradise
Christmas in Paradise
Puppies in Paradise
Halloween in Paradise
Treasure in Paradise
Fireworks in Paradise – *October 2017*
Beaches in Paradise – *June 2018*

Whales and Tails Cozy Mystery:
Romeow and Juliet
The Mad Catter
Grimm's Furry Tail
Much Ado About Felines
Legend of Tabby Hollow
Cat of Christmas Past
A Tale of Two Tabbies
The Great Catsby
Count Catula
The Cat of Christmas Present
A Winter's Tail
The Taming of the Tabby
Frankencat
The Cat of Christmas Future – *November 2017*
The Cat of New Orleans – *February 2018*

Seacliff High Mystery:
The Secret
The Curse
The Relic
The Conspiracy
The Grudge
The Shadow
The Haunting – *September 2017*

Sand and Sea Hawaiian Mystery:
Murder at Dolphin Bay
Murder at Sunrise Beach
Murder at the Witching Hour
Murder at Christmas
Murder at Turtle Cove
Murder at Water's Edge
Murder at Midnight – *October 2017*

Writers' Retreat Southern Seashore Mystery:
First Case
Second Look
Third Strike
Fourth Victim – *October 2017*
Fifth Night – *January 2018*

Rescue Alaska Paranormal Mystery:
Finding Justice – *November 2017*

A Tess and Tilly Mystery:
The Christmas Letter – *December 2017*

Road to Christmas Romance:
Road to Christmas Past

Chapter 1

Tuesday, October 24

Talk about déjà vu. One year ago tonight, on October 24, I, Caitlin Hart, attended a book club at Coffee Cat Books. One year ago tonight, a storm blew in and, very much like tonight, thunder and lightning created a spooky backdrop just above the horizon. I glanced out the huge picture window my best friend Tara O'Brian and I had installed when we'd remodeled the old cannery to open the coffee bar/bookstore/cat lounge. The pumpkin-scented candles Tara lit earlier in the evening flickered, creating a warm and cozy feeling when coupled with the roaring fire in the floor-to-ceiling fireplace we'd built into the reading room and cat lounge.

Even with the warmth of the room, I couldn't help but notice that the sky was dark with heavy clouds and the sea appeared angry as wind whipped its surface creating waves and white caps as far as the eye could see. The storm seemed to be inching closer to shore as the minutes ticked by and I wondered if we shouldn't call our discussion of Mary Shelley's classic *Frankenstein* to a close in favor of sending everyone home.

I glanced at Tara, who was leading the discussion. She was certainly in her element. Her face mirrored her happiness as she discussed the novel while fingering the necklace her boyfriend, Dr. Parker Hamden, had given her. I was happy Tara had found a man worthy of her love. She was such an awesome person, but before Parker came along she seemed to have hopped from one failed relationship to the next.

I thought about the cute Halloween costume Tara was making for Parker's niece, Amy. Tara had spent a ton of time on it, making sure every detail was absolutely perfect. Personally, I didn't think a child's costume warranted quite so much attention, but Tara seemed to really be in to the whole surrogate-mother thing. Amy was currently living with Parker while her mother was in prison. I wasn't certain what Amy's mother had done to land herself in so much trouble, but Parker had never mentioned it and I'd decided it wasn't any of my business, so I'd never asked.

Tara stopped speaking as thunder rolled in from the sea, shaking the shop, which was perched on the end of the wharf.

"That one sounded close," I commented as the lights flickered.

"I heard the storm is supposed to be a strong one, but it should pass quickly," Giselle Bowman, one of our regular book club members, informed us.

"I could use a bathroom break as long as the conversation's been interrupted anyway," Barbara Jenkins, a stay-at-home mom with two children, said.

"I'll second that," Stephanie Abrams and Alice Jones both voiced at the same time.

Tara looked at the clock on the wall. "Okay; we'll take a twenty-minute break. There are coffee and cookies in the other room. If Giselle is correct and the storm is going to blow through quickly we can finish our discussion after the break. If it looks like the storm is going to linger we'll break for the night."

Everyone other than Tara and I got up and wandered into the bookstore section of the building, where the coffee counter had been stocked with the coffee and cookies Tara had mentioned. I had to hand it to her; she was really embracing the Halloween spirit this year. Not only had she made three different types of cookies, all with a Halloween theme, but the entire bookstore was decorated from top to bottom, giving the space a magical feeling that made me want to abandon the book we were discussing and play make-believe with Tara's minivillage.

"Everyone seems to be enjoying the discussion," I commented as we watched the storm roll in.

"It's a great novel. You can't help but both fear and feel empathy for the monster. I've seen the movie, which I'll admit caused me more than a few tears, but as I read the novel, I found myself experiencing the pain and emptiness of living in a world where you'd never fit in."

"It sounds like you bonded with the monster."

Tara glanced at me. "Yeah, I guess I did. We all want to know who we are, why we are, and exactly where we came from. We all want to feel like we belong."

I took Tara's hand in mine as lightning crisscrossed through the sky. "It sounds as if you've been talking to Sister Mary again." Tara had been struggling with some issues as a result of learning that not only were the mother and father she had always believed to be her real parents had adopted her, but her actual parents were a nun and the man who had kidnapped her when she was just a girl.

"I have been speaking to her," Tara confirmed as the sound of thunder grew closer. "When I first discovered my real parentage I was surprised but not really upset about it, but the more time I've had to think about it the more I realize I have questions and issues I need to work out. Sister Mary has been so great. She's been patient and kind and has answered all my questions despite the fact that I can tell it's painful for her to revisit that part of her life."

"Sister Mary is awesome. You've always liked and admired her, while you never felt you fit in with your family. I know it must be hard having such a huge secret to keep, but I'd think you'd be happy you finally know the truth."

"I'm happy to know the truth and I'm happy to know Mary is my mother."

"But you're worried that you also carry the genes of your father," I realized.

Tara squeezed my hand as the storm grew closer. "Spending time with Amy has made me realize I very much want to have children of my own someday. I think I'd be a good mother, but I have to wonder if there isn't some latent evil residing in my genes."

I was about to respond when Paula Wainwright, one of our longtime book club members, interrupted. "Excuse me," she said, holding up her phone. "I'm sorry to bother you, but I need to make a call. My cell is dead. Would you mind if I used the phone in your office?"

"Certainly; help yourself," I answered. "The light switch is just to the right of the door when you enter."

A clap of thunder shook the building as the dark sky lit up with streaks of lightning overhead.

"Wow. That was really close. I hope we don't lose power," Tara said as we walked closer to the large windows and looked out over the dark sea. The heavy clouds blocked the light from the moon, making it hard to see, but the white-capped waves and lightning on the horizon were hard to miss.

"I'd be surprised if we don't, the way things are shaping up, but I think it's too late now to send everyone home." I paused as a clap of thunder echoed through the building. "It's safer in the bookstore than it would be on the road."

"I agree. Letting everyone go at this point would be a bad idea. The roads will be treacherous once the rain starts, which it looks as if it will be any minute."

"Yeah. It looks like it could get bad." My heart was beginning to pound as bolts of lightning neared. "We should probably step away from the window. In fact, we should tell everyone to move to the center of the building."

"That's probably a good idea. I had no idea the storm would be so strong. The way the building is shaking, I wouldn't be surprised if we don't end up with substantial wind damage."

"Let's just hope we don't blow away altogether."

A bolt of lightning hit the water just outside the window we were looking through. Tara and I screamed and jumped back. We were the only two in the cat lounge at that point. The others were either in line for the bathroom or gathered around the coffee bar, chatting among themselves. I grabbed Tara's hand and she squeezed mine in return. The lights flickered once again and then went out, plunging the store into darkness. It took just a moment for my eyes to adjust to the dim light provided by the fire. Thunder and strong winds shook the building as lightning flashed overhead. Gusts of blustery air whistled through the cracks in the doorway, adding to the eeriness of the darkened room.

"Cait, Tara, are you in here?" one of the book club members called from the doorway.

"Yes, we're here," Tara called back. "Let's all gather in here, where we have some light, but stay away from the windows."

The women filed back into the room one by one. We huddled together as the building shook so hard I was certain it was going to collapse on us. Several of the women were praying softly, while others simply clung to one another for comfort. After what seemed like hours the storm blew over and the wind died down.

"That was a bad one," said Jane Warton, a nurse at the local hospital.

"The worst I've ever seen," Sarah Frost agreed.

"Is everyone okay?" I asked.

There were general murmurs throughout the room that, while the women were shook up a bit, no one was physically injured.

The power was still out, so we all agreed it was best to break for the night now that the worst of the storm had passed. Tara cautioned everyone to drive safely and the women began to disperse. Tara and I banked the fire and began gathering our things to leave as well. Except for the light that had been provided by the fire and candles, it was pitch-black inside the store, so we figured we'd come in early the next morning to clean up. Once we'd extinguished the flames from the candles we opened the front door and looked out into the pouring rain.

"Paula Wainwright's car is still here," Tara pointed out.

"Maybe she got a ride with someone," I suggested.

"Maybe, but I would think she'd have said something to us if that was her plan." Tara was right. "Do you remember seeing her with the others?" she asked.

I thought about it. "Not specifically, but it was dark and everyone left shortly after the worst of the storm blew through. She did ask to use the phone in the office. We should check to make sure she isn't still in the building before we lock up."

Tara took out her cell phone and turned on her flashlight app. We walked side by side down the hallway, calling out Paula's name. The bathroom door was open, so we knew she wasn't in there. Then we searched the office, but it was empty as well.

"Maybe the storeroom?" Tara asked.

"We may as well look," I answered.

The windowless room was not only pitch-black except for the light provided by the cell phone flashlight, but it was stacked with boxes that were as many as four high around the room.

"Paula, are you in here?" I called.

There was no answer.

"She must have gotten a ride with one of the others," Tara said.

"Yeah. There wouldn't be any reason for her to come in here in the first place," I agreed. I was about to close the door when a large cat shot between my legs and entered the room. "What the heck? Where did you come from?" I turned to Tara. "We did close the front door, right?"

"I thought we did, but you know how it sometimes doesn't latch tight. It could have blown open. There are still some pretty strong gusts blowing through."

I looked in to the dark interior of the room. "Here, kitty. We need to go and I don't want to lock you in, so come on out."

"Meow."

I could hear the cat moving around in the back of the room, but he must be behind the stack of boxes because I couldn't see him. "I'll see if I can get him," I said to Tara. "Shine the light toward that stack of boxes in the back. I think he's behind them."

Tara did as I'd asked and I walked slowly through the storeroom, careful not to trip on anything. I could still hear the cat behind the boxes, so once I reached the back of the room I scooted around behind them. The light from Tara's phone didn't quite reach where I was now, but I could see something lying on the ground. I bent down to see if I could feel what it was when my hand came into contact with a human face.

"Tara, I think you'd better get over here. Bring the light."

"Did you find the cat?"

"I did. And something else as well."

I could hear Tara moving slowly through the room so as not to stumble over anything. I heard her gasp when she finally worked her way around to the spot where I was kneeling.

"Oh God. What happened?"

Paula was lying in a pool of blood. There was a large knife sticking out of her chest.

"I don't know. She doesn't have a pulse. Call Finn."

Chapter 2

Ryan Finnegan—Finn to his friends—was both the resident deputy for Madrona Island and my new brother-in-law. Tara and I had decided to wait in the car for him to arrive. There was nothing we could do for Paula and we didn't want to wait in the dark bookstore with the body of a woman who had been alive just thirty minutes ago.

I slipped out into the rain when Finn pulled up. Tara and I ran the short distance through the downpour toward the front door. Once the three of us were inside Finn asked us to show him to the body.

"What happened?" he asked a few minutes later as he stooped over the body.

"I don't know," I replied. "We were having our regular book club meeting when the storm blew in. It was a lot more intense than we thought it was going to be, so we decided to take a break until it passed. Paula asked to use the phone in the office, so I told her to go ahead and do it. We didn't realize she was missing until Tara and I were ready to leave and we saw her car was still in the lot. We both agree, after really stopping to think about it, that we don't remember seeing her after she left to use the phone."

"Who all was here?" Finn asked as he examined the body with a gloved hand.

"There were twelve of us, including Tara and me," I answered. "Paula, Giselle Bowman, Barbara Jenkins, Stephanie Abrams, Rachael Steinway, Jane Warton, Sarah Frost, Alice Jones, Martha Greyson, and Gwen Peterman."

"Did anyone else leave the group after Paula went to use the phone?" Finn asked.

"Yes. We'd all decided to take a break to use the bathroom and share the cookies Tara had brought. Tara and I were in the cat lounge together." I glanced at Tara. "We don't know who might have been where once the discussion broke up."

"Maybe someone came in through the exterior door between the office and the alley," Tara suggested.

Finn stood up. "We can look. There isn't much I can do here until the medical examiner and crime scene get here. Do you have something to cover the body?"

Tara handed Finn a large Halloween-themed tablecloth.

"Let's talk in the other room. We'll check the exterior door in the office on our way through."

When we arrived Finn checked the door, which was locked from the inside.

"Does this mean one of the women at the book club is the killer?" Tara stammered.

It did look that way, but I couldn't think of a single club member I'd suspect of murdering someone in cold blood. It was dark, so I couldn't tell for certain, but I was willing to bet Tara was feeling as shaky and light-headed as I was.

Finn grabbed a notepad and pen from the desk and suggested we head into the coffee bar so we wouldn't accidentally tamper with anything should the office turn out to have been the scene of the murder.

"So let's talk about the knife. Do you recognize it?" Finn began.

"Yes," Tara answered. "We sometimes use it to open boxes. The last time I saw it before tonight it was lying on the long work counter in the back room."

Finn jotted down some notes. "Okay, now that we've established the knife was already on the property and therefore didn't belong to the killer, it most likely won't tell us much unless we can pull some prints. I'll wait for the crime scene guys to do that. Tell me about the victim."

"She's been coming to the bookstore almost since we opened and I know she's lived on the island for about three years," Tara responded.

"She recently separated from her husband and has been working at the temp agency," I added.

"Children?" Finn asked.

"No. Not as far as I know," I answered.

"So tell me about the husband."

"His name is Henry," I said. "He's a good-looking man who I would estimate to be in his late thirties or early forties. He's an accountant who works for Calvin and Coleman. I think Paula said he had an apartment over in the Harthaven complex on Fourth Street. I don't know which unit, but I'm sure it would be easy to find out."

Finn jotted down a few notes. "Do you know why the couple separated?"

"Paula said he had a woman on the side," I said. "I guess there've been others, but Paula told me she'd finally had enough. I know Henry didn't take the separation well. If he were here I'd consider him the prime suspect, but because he wasn't I don't see how he could have done it."

"And who, out of the women who were here, would you consider to be a suspect?" Finn asked.

I thought about it before I replied. "No one. Paula seemed to get along with everyone."

"I agree." Tara nodded. "I can't believe any of the women in the club would have done such a thing."

Finn sat back on the sofa where we'd gathered to wait. "Well, someone stuck a knife in the woman's chest and because there's no sign anyone entered the store after the last book club member did, I have to assume one of the other nine women did it. Why don't you tell me what you know about each of them?"

"Okay," I said. "Giselle Bowman is around thirty, single, and an avid reader. This is the third book club reading she's participated in. She volunteers at the library on Tuesdays and waits tables three days a week at the Driftwood Café."

"And how would you classify her relationship with the decedent?"

"I don't think they were friends outside the book club, but they seemed to get along okay here. I didn't pick up any tension between them," I answered. I looked at Tara.

"They seemed to get along just fine," she seconded.

"Who else was here tonight?" Finn asked.

"Barbara Jenkins is a stay-at-home mom with two children, both preschool age," Tara began. "She's also around thirty and I think she and Paula both participate in community theater. In fact, it seems to me Paula was the one who brought Barbara to book club for the first time about a year ago. They seemed to get along well."

Tara glanced at me and I jumped in with the next book club member. "Stephanie Abrams is around forty and currently single, although I seem to remember she's divorced. She's a legal secretary at Brown and Bidwell. I don't think she was friends with Paula outside of book club, but I can't say that for certain. Stephanie is friends with Rachael Steinway, though. Rachael is also around forty, married, with three children all of whom are in their teens. Stephanie and Rachael belong to the same gardening club. I know that because they talked about their gardens quite frequently during last spring's book club."

"And their relationship with Paula?" Finn asked.

"I think they got along fine. I guess I would classify them as acquaintances. In fact, as far as I know, the only woman Paula was friends with outside book club other than Barbara was Jane Warton. Jane and Paula would meet for dinner before book club every now and then. Jane is a nurse at the hospital. She has funky hours, so she doesn't make every book club meeting, but she shows up often enough to keep up with the discussion. Jane's single with no children. She's also around thirty."

I waited while Finn scribbled on his notepad.

"And Sarah Frost?" Finn asked.

"Sarah Frost and Gwen Peterman are sisters," Tara answered. "Both are in their fifties; both are widows and have grown children who don't live on the island. Gwen's a math teacher at the high school and Sarah works for an accounting firm in Harthaven. They seem to be good friends as well as sisters. I'm not certain if they knew Paula outside of book club, but I've never noticed any tension between them. The only other women who were here tonight were Alice Jones and Martha Greyson. Alice is married with two young children. She's a teacher's aide part time. I guess she's maybe twenty-five or -six and is the nicest person you'd ever want to meet. Martha Greyson is in her early sixties. She moved to the island four years ago after she retired from teaching. She's a sweet lady I'm sure would never hurt anyone."

Finn's phone rang and we paused for him to answer it. When he hung up he turned back to us. "The sheriff's boat is about to dock. I think this will take a while. If the two of you want to go on home I can lock up for you."

I glanced at Tara, who nodded.

"Okay, thanks. I am tired. Will you call me in the morning?"

"I will. You should plan to be closed for a couple of days. I know you're busy on the weekends, so I'll try to have this wrapped up so you can reopen on Friday. If not Friday, then Tuesday." Finn knew we were closed on Sundays and Mondays.

"Okay," Tara said. "I'd hate to be closed for a whole week and would greatly appreciate it if the team could be done in time for us to open for the weekend, though I do understand that you need to protect the crime scene. I hope you find out who did it."

"Yeah. Me too. If you think of anything at all that could be relevant call or text me."

The cat that had alerted me to Paula's body had disappeared as mysteriously as he'd appeared. In my experience, the cats that were linked to murders always stuck around until the killer was found. I supposed if this cat was supposed to help me, he'd find his way to my cabin, so I hugged Tara good-bye and slipped into my car. I wanted to call my boyfriend, Cody West, but he'd been in Tampa Bay working on his training project for the SEALs and would most likely be fast asleep with the time difference. He was due to return to the island on Thursday, and if he knew about the murder he'd just be worried, so I decided to wait until he got back to fill him in. Of course, when he called me even before I got home, I realized I wasn't the only one on the island he was in touch with. It was probably my sister Siobhan who'd called Cody right after I'd called Finn.

"Hey, Cody," I answered after pulling over to the side of the road. The thunder and lightning had passed, but it was still pouring rain, which made it much too dangerous to talk and drive at the same time.

"I heard what happened. Are you okay?"

"I'm fine. I'm on my way home. Finn is at the bookstore and the crime scene guys were just arriving as I left. I don't suppose we'll know anything for a day or two."

I heard Cody let out a loud sigh. "I wish I could be there with you, but I really can't leave here until I finish briefing the top brass. Unfortunately, that's been moved from tomorrow until Thursday, which means I won't be home until Friday."

I felt a stab of disappointment but didn't want to make it harder on him than it already was. "That's okay. I'm fine."

"Are you planning on investigating this one?"

I let out a long sigh. "I don't know. I'm hoping Finn will handle it on his own this time. The number of possible suspects is limited to the nine other women in the store at the time of the murder. It shouldn't be too difficult to find out which of them stabbed Paula."

"Has a cat shown up?"

"Yes and no. There was a beautiful brown cat in the storeroom when we found the body, but he seems to have disappeared. I'm not sure if he'll show up again or not. I thought I'd go by to talk to Tansy tomorrow. Right now, I just want to get home and cuddle up by the fire with Max."

Cody paused before responding. "I can't believe I'm jealous of a dog."

I smiled. "Nothing against Max, but I wish it was you I was going to be cuddling with too. I've really missed you."

"I know. Me too. But this will be it until after the first of the year. I feel like we're almost done despite the fact that things are taking longer than I'd planned. In fact, I hope to have things completely finished by next spring, June at the latest. Once it's over, I'll need to train a group to actually implement it. What we've come up with is good. Really good. I think we'll save a lot of lives."

"Then it'll all be worth it." I glanced out the windshield, which was beginning to fog up. "I should get going. I'm sitting on the side of the road in a downpour. I can call you when I get home, or if it's too late we can just talk tomorrow."

"No, call me when you get home. I want to make sure you made it safely."

I hung up and restarted my car, turned the windshield wipers on high and the heater to defrost. Then I pulled slowly back onto the road and limped my way back to my oceanfront cabin on the peninsula, where my Aunt Maggie owned an estate. The Hart family was one of the twelve founding families of Madrona Island, who had divided the land among themselves. One of the plots of land my ancestor ended up with was the center third of the peninsula on the southwest end of the island. To this day, that peninsula is home to three estates, all owned by descendants of the original twelve. Aunt Maggie owned the middle third and I lived in a guest cabin situated right on the beach. Mr. Parsons lives on the estate to the south of us and Cody, who has been looking out for the elderly man, has an apartment on the third floor of his huge house. To our north was an estate owned by Francine Rivers, who helped to keep an eye on Mr. Parsons when Cody wasn't around. I checked in on Mr. Parsons on a regular basis too as I always have; in the Hart family, friends are like family and family are friends.

When I arrived at the cabin it was dark, but I could see Max looking out the window. The poor guy. I hated the fact that he'd been home alone while thunder and lightning had put on a show overhead.

I got out of the car and ran to the covered porch. I was about to open the door when I noticed the same brown cat I'd seen in the bookstore sitting under the swing.

"How in the heck did you get all the way over here in a storm?"

"Meow."

I picked the cat up and looked him in the eye. "Never mind. I know there are things that happen that can't be explained. Come on, I'll introduce you to Max."

Chapter 3

Wednesday, October 25

I got up early the next morning to take Max for a run. I'd been so busy lately that the dog hadn't been getting the attention he deserved. When Cody was in town he would often take Max to work with him at the *Madrona Island News*, but with him out of town poor Max had been forced to spend the day on his own.

The storm that had battered the island had passed, but I'd heard there was another one on the way. The beach was littered with debris washed up when the high waves pounded the shore. I ran along the water's edge, where the sand was the firmest, while Max ran ahead of me, chasing the seagulls that had arrived to look for their morning meal.

I paused as a bald eagle flew overhead, watching as he circled a few times and then landed on a branch on top of a tree that hugged the shoreline. He looked so regal as he looked out over the beach in search of his next meal. There were plenty of dead fish up on the shore this morning, so I doubted any of the birds in the area would go hungry.

I was glad I'd decided to take a run this morning. Not only was it good for Max, it was good for me. I'd tossed and turned all night as the image of Paula's dead body filled my mind despite my best efforts to focus on something else. I'm not sure why it seemed that every murder that occurred on the island somehow involved me, but being plunged into one investigation after another had left me feeling weary. I hoped this one would be wrapped up by Halloween and then, hopefully, I could enjoy Thanksgiving and Christmas with my friends and family without having the violent death of someone I knew and cared about overshadowing the festivities.

I knew Aunt Maggie planned to host Thanksgiving this year because my mom and my sister Cassie were still living in their tiny apartment. There would be eighteen of us for dinner: In addition to myself, Maggie was inviting my mom and her boyfriend Gabe; my two brothers, Danny and Aiden; Cassie and our older sister Siobhan and Finn; Tara and Parker and Amy; Cody, Mr. Parsons, and Francine; Maggie's best friend Marley; Sister Mary; and, of course, Father Kilian, who wouldn't be Father Kilian for much longer. He'd retired at the end of May and planned to officially leave the priesthood at the end of the year so he could marry Maggie the following spring. I was really looking forward to having everyone I loved together to give thanks for all we had.

I wanted to see Tansy that morning, so I called Max back from the wave he was chasing. I loved this time of the morning, when the sun was just beginning to peek over the horizon and the day held the promise of endless possibilities. There's something about watching the sun rise in the sky as the ocean laps onto the shore that calms the mind and feeds the soul in a way little else can. I felt very blessed to live on the beautiful island of my birth and gave thanks every day for the richness I found in life and the people I'd been given to share it with.

I was almost back to the cabin when I noticed something floating in the water. It looked like a glass ball, and at first I thought it was a glass fisherman's float. I'd found a lot of those over the years in a variety of colors. But then I realized the size as well as the color of the orb was different. Although the water was freezing, I took off my shoes, rolled up my pants, and waded out to retrieve it. Luckily, it wasn't that far out, so I was able to retrieve it without getting completely soaked.

******

"The cat's name is Frank," Tansy informed me as we shared a pot of tea later that morning.

"Seems like an odd name for a cat."

Tansy shrugged. "I'm afraid I'm not in charge of these things. All I can tell you is that Frank has been sent to help you figure out what led to Paula Wainwright's death."

"We know she was stabbed in the heart with a big old knife. Now we just need to figure out who stabbed her." I paused to take a sip of my tea.

"Would you like another muffin?" Tansy offered. "I know they're your favorite."

"Yes, please." I wanted to ask how it was Tansy always seemed to have a freshly baked batch of my favorite muffins on hand when I stopped by, but I supposed her answer would be as vague as everything else she said to me. "This case has me feeling unsettled," I said after accepting the muffin. "There were only twelve people in the bookstore last night, Tara and me, along with Paula, and nine other women. The back door was locked from the inside and if someone had come in through the front we would have seen them from the cat lounge, where the book club was being held. That means one of the other nine women had to have killed Paula. I've known all of them for at least a year, many longer. While I can't claim to know them well, I know them well enough to say none of them strike me as the sort to be a cold-blooded killer. They're all very nice and seem to get along with one another. Many of them are involved in other groups on the island. The whole thing doesn't make sense."

"At times, when faced with an impossible set of circumstances, it's necessary to question our assumptions."

"Question our assumptions? What does that mean?"

Tansy just smiled and topped off my tea. I could see she wasn't going to give me anything else to go on. At least Frank was waiting for me back at my cabin. I was really hoping he'd come through, as the cats before him had.

"I guess that smile means I have to figure it out for myself."

"Which I know you will. You're very special, Caitlin. I sense you have a gift even you haven't yet discovered."

"A gift?" I groaned. "If there's one thing I've learned in my life a gift isn't always *a gift*. Which reminds me…" I reached into my backpack and pulled out the clear, seamless glass ball I'd found earlier. "What do you make of this? I found it in the water near my cabin. When I first saw it I thought it was a fisherman's float, but now I'm not so sure."

Tansy took it into her hands, frowning as she turned it over and over, examining every side. "I agree; this isn't a float." Tansy looked up at me. "Can I keep this for a while?"

I shrugged. "Sure. If it's a crystal ball of some kind it's better off in your hands than mine." I took the last sip of my tea. "Thank you for the muffins and the conversation. I need to go, but if you come up with any insights you can share please call or text."

"I will and Godspeed."

I left the house Tansy shared with Bella, her partner in both life and business, and headed to Finn's office. I had no idea where to even begin with this investigation, but I figured finding out what Finn already knew was as good a place to start as any. Luckily, he was in his office working on his computer when I arrived.

"I was just going to call you," he greeted me.

"Here I am, saving you the trouble. Any news?"

"Some. Have a seat. Coffee?"

"No, thanks. I just had tea with Tansy."

Finn opened a file folder on his desk and began to speak. "Paula Wainwright was stabbed in the chest with an upward thrust. Based on the angle and location, it appears as if the killer was standing in front of her. The knife entered her body just below the sternum and was thrust upward toward her heart. In my experience, men are more likely to thrust in a downward or overhand motion, while women thrust upward."

"Which brings us back to the idea that it must have been a book club member who killed Paula."

"I'm afraid so."

"What else do you know?" I asked.

"Not a lot. We know Paula was killed in the vicinity of where the body was found. We don't know why she was in the storeroom. You said she went into the office to use the phone, so initially, I figured the killer assaulted her there and dragged her into the storeroom, but we've gone over the office with a fine-tooth comb and haven't found any evidence of a struggle. We also didn't find any defensive wounds on the body, which indicates she most likely was surprised by her attacker and didn't put up a fight."

"Maybe she was speaking to someone who grabbed the knife and stabbed her before she knew what hit her."

"Perhaps. We did find Paula's fingerprints on the phone, so we're assuming she made the call she intended to before she headed into the storeroom. I requested your phone records; there was a call made from the bookstore at eight twenty-six last evening to a number associated with a burner cell. I assume Paula's the only one who might have used the phone at that time."

"As far as I know," I said.

"My current theory is that she went into the office and made her call. When she left the office to return to the group she either met the killer in the hallway and was lured into the storeroom, where she was killed, or she heard something in the storeroom and went in to check it out."

"I hate this case."

"I know." Finn's eyes softened.

"It makes no sense. I just can't believe any of the book club members would do such a thing. It seems so barbaric."

"I'm sorry this happened in your store, but I've been doing this job long enough to know very nice people sometimes do horrible things."

I groaned in frustration but didn't otherwise respond.

"Last night you mentioned Paula was divorcing her husband because he had another woman. Do you happen to know who the other woman was?"

I shook my head. "No. Paula never said. I suppose you can ask Henry."

"I did and he denied having an affair. He said he loved his wife and had always been faithful to her, but she was paranoid and tended to create evidence that he'd strayed where none existed. I asked him why he moved out of the house he shared with her and he said she'd kicked him out because he was having the affair he swears he isn't having. He also said this wasn't the first time she'd kicked him out."

I frowned. "That's odd. He has to be lying."

"Maybe, but I didn't get the sense he was. He seemed genuinely distraught when I told him Paula was dead. I suppose he could have been sleeping around, but at this point I'm giving him the benefit of the doubt."

I narrowed my gaze. Paula didn't seem the type to make things up, but I didn't know her all that well, so I supposed she *could* have issues with paranoia. "Did Henry say anything else that might help with the case?"

"He said that before he moved out, Paula had been getting calls at odd hours. Sometimes her cell would ring in the middle of the night. He asked her who was calling and she always said it was a wrong number. He admitted that could be true; he never heard Paula having a conversation with the caller. She'd simply pick up the phone, listen, and then hang up. But Henry thought the calls strange enough to mention."

I rested my head in my hands. This was giving me a headache. "Okay, so Paula was getting strange calls. She was paranoid that her husband was having an affair he claims he wasn't having. Maybe someone was messing with Paula—calling her and telling her Henry was being unfaithful."

"But why would someone do that?"

I shrugged. "Who knows why anyone does anything? It's just one possible explanation, but it could have played out that way. It's possible there was someone who wanted to break Paula and Henry up for some reason."

"Or maybe Paula had a mental health issue," Finn pointed out.

"Or maybe Henry really was cheating," I countered.

"I don't suppose we're going to figure this out without more to go on."

"Can we trace the calls made to Paula's phone?"

"If we can isolate the numbers. I'll pull her phone records to see what I can find."

I took a deep breath and let it out slowly. "Okay. Maybe the phone records will provide a clue. In the meantime, what can I do? How can I help?"

"I plan to interview every woman who was at the book club last evening. It might help if you did the same. Maybe Tara can help you. You know these women. They may tell you things they won't tell me. Maybe Paula told someone she was close to who her husband was sleeping with. If we can find who she is and she admits to the affair at least that will answer the question of whether Henry's lying."

"Yeah, okay, I can do that. Anything else?"

"I'd like to escort you and Tara to the bookstore today. I want you to look around to see if you notice anything missing or out of place. You'll need to look carefully but not touch anything."

"I can do that. I'm sure Tara will as well. But I feel so conflicted about this. I want the killer to be found, but when I start to imagine it might be one of the nine suspects we currently have my stomach begins to churn and my legs feel wobbly. I'm really having a hard time dealing with the fact that someone I know fairly well is a murderer."

"I know, Cait, and I'm sorry. I'll try to get this case wrapped up as quickly as possible. I'm hoping the crime scene guys will come up with some conclusive physical evidence. At this point the murder doesn't appear to have been premeditated. If I had to guess I'd say the killer simply took advantage of the noise and confusion caused by the storm and acted on impulse."

"Yeah, but why do it there? Why not wait until Paula went home, where there wouldn't be any witnesses? I guess it could have been a crime of passion. Maybe someone lured Paula into the storage area to have a chat with her, they argued, then the killer just happened to see the knife and used it without thinking about the consequences."

"That's possible. I'm hoping we can find out for sure."

Finn called Tara, who said she could be at the bookstore in an hour. I decided to go home to get Frank. In the past, the cats seemed to have the answers even before the human investigators had a chance to figure out what the questions were. Finn didn't blink an eye when I told him my intention, which made me appreciate him even more than I already did. I couldn't wait for there to be a little Finn running around, getting into everything. It had been four months since Finn and Siobhan had married and I knew they'd planned to start trying for a baby right away. I'd been expecting to hear an announcement for a while now, although Siobhan would probably want to wait until the perfect moment to tell me I was going to be an aunt.

Chapter 4

Finn was already waiting in front of the bookstore and Tara was just getting out of her car when Frank and I showed up. The jack-o'-lantern that had greeted the book club members the previous evening had blown over and broken in half after it hit the planter box full of chrysanthemums Tara had planted a few weeks earlier. The flowers had weathered the storm better than I expected, but the colorful fall flag that had been hanging over the doorway was shredded beyond recognition and the awning over the entry was going to need to be replaced.

"Okay, so we're going to walk through the store one room at a time," Finn explained as he handed Tara and me each a set of gloves. "The gloves are a precaution, though it'll be best if you don't touch anything at all. If you see something that looks odd, out of place, or missing, tell me and I'll take a closer look."

Finn opened the front door and the three of us walked into the bookstore. Everything looked perfectly normal, except for the fact that the cups and dirty plates from the previous evening's snack were still sitting on the coffee bar.

"You might want to bag the cups," I suggested. "Just in case you need DNA at some point in the future."

"Good idea. I'm surprised the crime scene guys didn't already do that."

"Have they left the island?" Tara asked.

"Yes. They've completed their investigation for the time being. I'm supposed to keep the crime scene secure until they release it, which, as I explained last night, will be in a couple of days at least."

Tara and I walked around the main part of the building, which housed the coffee bar and bookstore. Other than the remnants left from the book club meeting nothing appeared to be out of place. We took our time, looking at every shelf just in case someone had left something behind. We searched the floor and even opened the cabinets behind the coffee bar. It didn't appear that anything was out of place. Once we finished in the bookstore we headed into the cat lounge and reading room, where the actual club discussion had been held. The folding chairs were still arranged in a circle and the book Tara had been using was still open to the page where she'd left off. The floor needed to be swept and mopped after so many people with wet feet had tromped over it, but nothing looked unusual or out of place.

We finished in the cat lounge and headed to the office Tara and I used to take care of the business end of the bookstore. The room held a single desk with a phone, a computer and printer, a row of file cabinets, a bookshelf that held the binders where we kept information on our vendors and inventory, the pegs where we hung our purses and jackets, and two extra chairs that were positioned against the wall to allow for more than one occupant of the room at a time. At first glance, nothing looked out of place, but on further examination I noticed a single yellow leaf on the hardwood floor.

"I know I cleaned in here yesterday before the ladies came for book club," I said aloud.

"Yes," Tara acknowledged. "It looks fine."

"I know, but I did the floor too." I stooped over and picked up the leaf, only realizing after I'd done so that Finn had told me not to touch anything. I handed the leaf to him. "This leaf wasn't there before book club. I'm sure of it. I realize it could have been on the bottom of someone's shoe and was tracked in, but I don't think anyone was in the office before Paula came in to use the phone." I glanced at Tara. "Did you come in here after I cleaned?"

She shook her head. "I was busy setting up in the front."

"Can either of you think of anyone else who came down the hall for any reason?" Finn asked.

Both Tara and I paused to give Finn's question consideration, but after a bit we shook our heads.

"The women came in to the store one at a time," Tara began. "I greeted them and they went directly into the cat lounge. If someone had used the bathroom or gone into the office before the meeting started I would have known. Once everyone was here, I joined the women and we got started. No one left the group until we took our break after the storm arrived."

"Could someone have had a leaf stuck to her shoe the entire time and then tracked it into the office during the break?" I asked.

"Seems unlikely," Finn said as he held up the maple leaf, which he bagged. "There are times when a leaf is just a leaf, but I'll hang on to it just in case. Do you think it's possible one of the women opened the side door to allow someone to enter the office, then closed and locked it after they left?"

Tara and I agreed that could have happened. During the break, when everyone was wandering around, neither Tara nor I were keeping an eye on the movements of the others. If someone did sneak another person into the building, who did the sneaking, who did they grant access to, and why was access granted? And when did that happen, before or after Paula used the phone?

"Even though it's possible a book club member snuck someone in through the side door it seems unlikely to me," Tara said after a bit.

"I suppose Paula's death could have been premeditated, that one of the book club members arranged for help in killing her, but there's no way anyone could have known the storm would blow in, interrupting our discussion, or that Paula would ask to use the phone. It's all too random," I added.

"Maybe the leaf blew into the building through the front door and somehow managed to find its way into the office. Or maybe one of the crime scene guys tracked it in last night," Finn suggested.

"That seems more likely," I admitted.

"Okay; moving on from the leaf, do you notice anything else?" Finn asked.

I looked around the room, trying to compare it to the way it had looked when I'd last seen it, but as far as I could tell it looked pretty much the same. The phone had been pulled closer to the middle of the desk, but we already knew Paula had used it. Tara tended to keep the office clean and clutter-free, so there weren't any stacks of paperwork or loose file folders sitting around to be disrupted. There was a stack of yellow sticky notes on the desk and a dark blue pen I was certain hadn't been there the previous evening. Maybe Paula had needed to make a note.

Tara also looked around but didn't find anything out of place. After several minutes Finn led us down the hallway to the storeroom. My stomach began to churn as he opened the door. The stacks of boxes that had been organized in a specific fashion as inventory arrived were moved to the side of the room farthest away from where Paula's body had been found. There was a bloodstain on the floor and someone had used chalk to trace the outline of the body. I also saw numbered yellow flags around the room, I imagined to reference items gathered for evidence.

"It's really important that you not touch anything in here," Finn reminded us.

"Everything has been moved," Tara commented. "I'm not sure how we can pick out the differences between what the crime scene crew might have moved and what the killer might have altered."

"Yeah," I agreed. "It looks totally different in here. When I came in last night it was dark. There was a wall of boxes over there." I pointed. "Frank, the cat, ran behind the boxes, so I made my way across the room to get him. That's when I found Paula's body." I thought about the cat I'd brought with me but had left in the car. "Should I get Frank? You never know what he might have seen or might know."

"Get the cat," Finn agreed. "As crazy as it seems, those cats have helped in the past. But whatever you do, don't tell the other deputies about it. I don't want the sheriff to think I've lost my mind."

I went out to the car and grabbed the cat. Back in the bookstore, I set him on the floor and closed the door. The cat trotted directly toward the storage room, where Tara and Finn were waiting. He didn't even pause before he ran over to one of the cabinets we'd built to store breakables such as mugs and ceramic items we needed quick access to but didn't do as well as books in boxes. This cabinet was attached to the wall, along with five other identical cabinets in a row. Frank scratched at the door, which seemed to be firmly closed. I walked across the room and opened the door with my gloved hand. Inside were three shelves full of the pink Coffee Cat Books mugs we used for the coffee bar, two shelves of ocean-themed souvenirs we stocked for the visitors who came over on the ferry, and a shelf on the bottom where Tara had stored a toolbox with the hand tools we used for small repairs around the place.

"Okay, what are we looking for?" I asked the cat.

He batted at something under the bottom shelf. The space between it and the floor was about an inch in height and was covered by the door except for a narrow opening of perhaps a quarter inch in height. I supposed something such as a piece of paper or other equally thin object could have been dropped near the cabinet and ended up underneath it.

"If there's something under the cabinet I'm not sure how we'll get it," I said.

Finn lay down on the floor with a flashlight and peered under the cabinet. "I do see something. It looks like a paper from a pad of sticky notes." Finn stood up and looked around. He opened the toolbox and found a long screwdriver. Then he lay back down and used the screwdriver to get hold of the paper and pull it toward him. When he stood up he read it. "It just says *Amber*. There are two dates written under the name, April 12, 1999, and November 6, 2014. Does this mean anything to either of you?"

Tara and I both said it didn't.

"I noticed a pen on the desk," I said aloud. "And the stack of yellow sticky notes had been left on the center of the desk. I wonder if Paula made a note during her call. She might have had the note in her hand and dropped it as she passed this part of the room. I suppose if the note fell to the floor at just the right angle it could have ended up under the cabinet."

"Do you recognize Paula's handwriting?" Finn asked.

I looked at the note. "No. But it isn't mine or Tara's either."

"If Paula used the pad in the office to make this note we might be able to confirm it."

Finn headed to the door and Tara and I followed him back to the office. He scratched a pencil over the surface of the note on the top of the pad. The dates on the note we'd found were clearly recognizable.

"Okay, so Paula came into the office to use the phone after you decided to take a break. During the course of her call she had reason to jot down the name and the dates. Shortly after she completed her call she was murdered in the storeroom."

"Do you think the note and the murder are connected?" I asked.

"I don't know," Finn admitted. "But I intend to find out."

Chapter 5

"So what now?" Tara asked after Finn left. We were standing on the walkway in front of the bookstore because Finn had locked the door and replaced the crime scene tape.

"Finn suggested we speak to the women who attended book club individually. He's going to do the same thing, but he thinks they might be more open with us than they will be with him or one of the other men investigating the murder."

"Do you think any of them even knows about Paula yet?" Tara asked.

"Probably not. Finn has spoken to a few people, though, so maybe word has gotten around. I thought maybe we'd start with Jane and Barbara. They seemed to know Paula better than the others. Maybe there was something going on in Paula's life that would help to give us some perspective."

"That sounds like a good idea." Tara glanced at the front door. "I don't think this thing really hit me until we went back inside this morning. There was so much blood. I didn't remember there being so much blood."

I frowned. "The power was off last night, so we wouldn't have noticed the amount of blood, but there really was a lot of it. Doesn't it seem that if you were standing in front of someone and you stabbed them in the chest you would have blood spatter on your clothes?"

Tara's eyes grew wide. "It does seem like you'd get at least some blood on your clothes. In fact, if the killer actually penetrated Paula's heart there would be a lot of blood spatter. I suppose if it was on your skin, your hands, or your arms, you could wash it off. But your clothes?"

I took a moment to consider the idea. "It was pretty dark once the lights went off and everyone did have jackets with them. I suppose the killer could have had blood on her clothes but was able to slip her jacket on before anyone noticed."

"That would mean she didn't rejoin the group until after everyone else gathered to leave," Tara pointed out. "Do you remember if anyone was missing when we all huddled together during the worst of the storm?"

I thought about it. "I don't remember anyone being missing, but then, I didn't notice Paula was missing either, so who knows?"

Tara wiped a tear from the corner of her eye. "Up to this point this hasn't felt real. I knew it happened, but in a way it felt like a really bad dream. But when I walked into the storage room and saw all that blood it really hit me. I'm surprised I managed to get through it without passing out."

"I know what you mean. It was pretty intense. Why don't you follow me to my cabin? I'll drop off Frank and my car and we can ride together."

"Okay. I'll be right behind you."

******

Jane was home but scheduled to work a swing shift at the hospital, so we started with her. She asked us to meet her at her home, which was just a half mile from the hospital. She greeted us at the front door dressed casually in a pair of jeans and a sweatshirt. Jane was a petite woman with dark brown eyes, fair skin, and dark curly hair she wore in a ponytail. The red rim around her eyes gave evidence to the fact that she'd been crying. I stepped inside and wrapped her in a comforting hug.

"I can't believe this happened," Jane began. "I work in a hospital. I've seen a lot of horrible things. But this… This makes no sense."

"We agree," Tara said as she stepped in for a hug as well before the three of us headed into the main living area, where Jane indicated we should take a seat on the sofa. "The main reason we're taking to book club members today is to try to make sense of a situation that simply doesn't."

Jane sat down on a chair across from us. "Do you think someone from book club killed her?"

"We aren't sure," I said. "On the surface I can't think of a single person in the group who would. Still, the back door was locked from the inside and we didn't notice anyone come in or go out of the front door other than book club members. By the process of elimination, it seems someone from our group must have been the killer. Can you think of anyone Paula was having problems with?"

Jane hesitated, averting her eyes, which indicated to me that someone had come to mind.

"All we're doing right now is talking to people. If you know something it would be very helpful if you'd share it with us," I added.

"I'm not accusing anyone of anything, but I guess you heard Paula and Henry separated recently," Jane began.

"I had heard that," I confirmed.

"Paula believed Henry had been unfaithful," Jane continued. "At first I believed that to be true. I mean, why would she make it up? But after a couple of weeks her story began to change and become more complicated. After a bit I began to wonder."

"Change how?" I asked.

"Initially, Paula told me Henry was cheating on her with a woman he worked with. She said he'd been unfaithful before and she'd come to the end of her rope. She told me that she planned to kick him out of the house. In the beginning I supported her a hundred percent. I don't think any woman should feel she has to stay with a man who strays. But then she began to change her story."

"How?" I asked again.

"For one thing, the identity of the woman Henry was cheating with. Paula started off by telling me he was cheating with a woman he worked with, but then, about two weeks ago, she told me Henry was cheating with Giselle Bowman."

"Giselle?" I asked with surprise.

"I found it odd too. Paula's accusation against Giselle seemed to come out of nowhere. I asked Paula if she was sure and she told me that she'd seen them together. The whole idea felt off to me, but Giselle is extremely attractive and she's single and around the same age as Henry. I guess it isn't outside the realm of possibility that he'd be attracted to her. And Henry is fairly good-looking as well and has a good job and seems to have a fun and outgoing personality. I guess stranger things have happened. I mean, people have affairs all the time."

"You don't sound totally convinced despite your words," Tara commented.

"That's because I'm not. Like I said, something just felt off." Jane paused. "Based on conversations I'd had with Paula in recent weeks, it seemed she was dealing with something heavy. She's always tended toward mood swings, but lately she'd been depressed and distracted. I suppose finding out your husband is cheating on you would be enough to explain her overall mood, but it felt to me like there might be something more."

"Do you have any idea what that *something more* might be?" Tara asked.

"No. Not really. I know she was upset about the situation with Henry, but the fact that she seemed unsure about the details bothered me. Still, even though I'm really not sure how I feel about Paula's assertion that Henry was cheating with Giselle, if someone at the meeting did kill Paula I guess you should talk to her. If Giselle was cheating with Henry I guess that gives her motive to want Paula out of the way, and if she wasn't cheating with Henry but Paula was going around telling everyone she was, that might make her pretty mad."

I supposed Giselle did make a pretty good suspect. "Last night, after we announced the break, Paula went into the office to make a phone call. Do you remember seeing anyone else heading in that direction?"

"I went straight to the bathroom. I got there first and didn't see Paula at all. When I came out Barbara, Alice, and Stephanie were in line. I went back into the bookstore, where the others were having coffee. People were scattered around the room talking. I chatted with Gwen for a while, and I remember seeing Barbara with Martha. I don't specifically remember anyone being missing, but I wasn't looking for that either."

I hesitated before asking my next question. Finn hadn't told me not to mention the note we'd found in the storage room, but it felt like something he might not want publicized, "Did Paula ever mention someone named Amber?" I finally asked.

Jane frowned. "The name doesn't ring a bell. Do you think someone named Amber is involved in this?"

"Not necessarily. It's just a name that came up." I glanced at Tara. She didn't seem to have any additional questions. "I just have one last question. Do you happen to know when Paula and Henry got together?"

"I'm not sure when they met, but Paula mentioned a couple of months ago that they were coming up on their fifth wedding anniversary, although she wasn't sure they'd make it, based on the way things were going."

"So that would mean they were married in 2012?"

"That would be my assumption."

"Do you know if Paula was ever married before Henry?"

"She never mentioned it. Having said that, we usually discussed things like news, books we'd read, movies we wanted to see. We weren't the sort of friends who shared information about our lives prior to our meeting each other or even the really intimate details of our current lives." Jane paused, seeming to consider something. "I know you probably can't get access to her medical records, but you might want to ask Finn if he has. I can't say for certain, but in my opinion Paula seemed to be demonstrating symptoms normally seen in individuals with bipolar disorder. If she does suffer from it, she might not have been taking her meds."

"Thanks; we will," Tara said.

We spoke with Jane for a few more minutes, then headed to Barbara Jenkins's house. Barbara was involved in community theater with Paula, and though they didn't seem to be superclose friends, I knew they did get together socially. Next to Jane, we figured Barbara was the club member Paula would be most apt to confide in. Barbara, a woman of average height with short brown hair, greeted us at the door with a diaper slung over one shoulder.

"Please come in and ignore the mess," Barbara said. "Not only do I have my two- and four-year-olds, but today I'm watching my sister's two children, who are eight months and three years."

"Wow, you really have your hands full. We appreciate your taking the time to speak to us," Tara offered with a smile.

"I'm happy to help in any way I can. The older kids are watching cartoons in the den and I just finished putting the younger two down for naps, so I should have a few minutes to talk. Can I get you anything to drink?"

"No. Thank you," I answered. "We'll try to be brief so we don't take up too much of your time."

Tara started off by asking the usual questions regarding Paula's relationship with the other members of the book club. Barbara felt certain no one from the group could have killed Paula, that there had to be another explanation, though Tara reminded her that Paula *had* been killed, and in a closed environment, and asked her opinion of who in the group might have had a problem with her in the days before her death.

This time we weren't surprised when Barbara mentioned Giselle.

"When Paula told me Henry was cheating with Giselle I wasn't sure what to think about it. I started watching Giselle at the meetings and she seemed to be interacting with Paula in a normal manner. If I were having an affair with some woman's husband I'd think it might cause me to act awkwardly, be secretive, maybe even a little defensive, but Giselle seemed open and friendly to Paula whenever they exchanged words."

"So you think Paula might have been lying?" Tara asked.

"I wasn't sure at first, but about a week ago I mentioned to a friend of mine, who also knows Paula from the community theater, that she and Henry had split. She told me she'd heard about it and she said this wasn't the first time Paula had kicked Henry out. In fact, she told me that her husband and Henry knew each other from the adult basketball league they both played in. Henry told him this was the third time Paula had decided he was cheating and thrown him out. He also told his wife that Henry claimed he'd never cheated once since he'd married Paula."

I remembered Henry had told Finn the same thing.

"What do you think about all this?" I asked.

"After I spoke to my friend I began to think back over the various conversations I've had with Paula. It occurred to me that there were other situations when she seemed to get things wrong. I'm not sure I'd go so far as to say she was intentionally lying, but she definitely tended to remember things incorrectly. I began to wonder if somehow things regarding Henry and Giselle started as a misconception and spiraled into something with no basis in reality."

"As far as you know, did Giselle know what Paula suspected?" Tara asked.

Barbara shrugged. "I have no idea if Paula ever confronted her, but I don't think so. Giselle seemed fine last night. I didn't notice any tension between them. Wouldn't there have been tension if Paula had said something to her? You should ask Giselle. My feeling is that she'll be as surprised by all this as we are."

"I understand from speaking to some of the others that Paula has been acting odd lately," Tara commented.

"Yes, as I said, she seemed to be confused over the past couple of weeks."

"One of the people we spoke to suggested she might be bipolar."

Barbara frowned. "She never talked about anything like that, but it would explain a lot. Can't you speak to her doctor about it?"

"Finn would be the one to do that. I was just curious whether she'd ever mentioned being on medication to you," Tara explained.

"No. We never spoke of our medical issues with each other."

Tara paused, and I decided to change the direction of the conversation a bit. "After we took our break last night Paula asked to use the phone in the office. Did you see anyone else headed in that direction?"

"I went straight for the restroom but wasn't quick enough. Jane got there first, so I waited by the door. Alice got into line behind me and Stephanie was behind her. I didn't see Paula at all and the bathroom is in the same hallway as the office, so she must have either gone into the office while I was in the restroom or maybe she'd already gone inside the office and remained there until after I joined the others for coffee."

"And do you remember if anyone was missing from the main room when you returned?" I asked.

"I didn't pay all that much attention. I chatted with Martha for a bit and then Alice joined us when she got back from

71

the restroom. I also saw Jane talking to Gwen. I can't vouch for the others, but to be honest, I didn't know anything was going to happen so I wasn't exactly taking notes. I'm pretty sure everyone was around at the end, when we all gathered together to wait out the storm."

"Except Paula," Tara pointed out.

Barbara sighed. "Yes, except Paula. I guess if I didn't notice she wasn't with us I might not have noticed the killer was missing either. This is just so upsetting."

Tara reached out to squeeze Barbara's hand before asking her next question. "The way I remember it, Cait and I spoke to each other for a few minutes before Paula asked us if she could use the phone. If you headed directly to the restroom Paula must have gone into the office while you were inside. If Alice and Stephanie were in line they should have seen her go in there."

"I suppose," Barbara answered.

"I just have one last question," I spoke up. "Did Paula ever mention anyone named Amber to you?"

Barbara twisted her mouth as she considered the question. "No. The name doesn't ring a bell. Should it?"

"Not necessarily. It's just a name that came up and I wanted to ask about it."

Chapter 6

We thanked Barbara for her time and returned to Tara's car, sitting for a minute in front of the house to discuss the situation. We both felt we could eliminate Barbara and Jane as suspects. They seemed to have alibis and to really care about Paula. It sounded like there was a line at the bathroom at least initially, so chances were Paula had left the office and entered the storeroom after the lights went out. Of course, that didn't make any sense. We needed to ask Stephanie if anyone had gotten into line for the bathroom behind her. If not, it may have been empty before the power outage.

"It's lunchtime," Tara said. "Let's grab a bite to eat and then come up with a strategy for the afternoon. The sooner we get this wrapped up the sooner we can reopen the bookstore."

"I have stuff for sandwiches at home. Let's just head back there so we can talk without being overheard," I suggested.

Tara started her car and headed back to the peninsula. It was a warm autumn day, so maybe we could enjoy our lunch on the deck overlooking the ocean. It wouldn't be long before the warm days we'd been experiencing from time to time gave way to the cooler and shorter days of winter. I figured we should enjoy all the outdoor time we could while we had the chance to do so.

"So what do you think about the idea of Giselle and Henry?" Tara asked after we'd settled onto the deck with our lunch. The waves lapping onto the shore lent a calming effect to the otherwise tense topic we were discussing.

"Seems unlikely. Not that I really know either Henry or Giselle all that intimately to judge what they may be capable of, but Giselle hasn't been acting odd in the least around Paula. Come to think of it, Paula hadn't been acting all that odd either. You would think if she really believed Giselle had broken up her marriage she wouldn't even have wanted to be in the same room with her."

Tara took a sip of her soda. "I had a similar thought. The whole thing doesn't feel quite right to me. Maybe one of the others will have a different perspective. If one of the book club women did kill Paula someone must have seen something."

"I agree. Who should we try to speak to first?"

"I'm not sure. Almost everyone will be at work. We might catch Martha at home, and if Giselle is off today she might be available to speak to us as well. Let's start by calling the two of them and take it from there."

"Sounds like a plan. So, what do you make of the sticky note we found? If Paula jotted down the name *Amber* minutes before her death, it seems it must be a clue."

"Not necessarily," Tara countered. "Paula's death most likely wasn't even related to her call. If you think about it, the person she called couldn't have been the killer unless Paula was calling one of the women at the book club meeting, but that doesn't make any sense."

"That's true." I nodded. "Amber probably isn't a clue, though I'm still curious."

"Me too. We'll keep asking about her. Maybe Paula mentioned her to someone she spoke to that evening. If not, maybe Henry will know."

∗∗∗∗∗∗

Martha Grayson wasn't only at home and not busy when we called but was anxious to speak to us. She'd heard about Paula's death from Gwen Peterman and had been fretting about it all day. She was the only retired member of the book club and therefore the one with the most time on her hands.

"Please come in," Martha said at the door of her small, immaculate home. "I just can't believe what happened to poor Paula. Who would do such a thing?"

"We don't know, but we're trying to find out," Tara replied.

"Let's sit in the kitchen. I made us some tea to go with the cookies I baked earlier. I haven't been able to relax a minute since I heard."

Tara and I sat down at the small, round table that was placed in a nook just off the kitchen. The cookies were chocolate chip, my favorite, so I took two even though we'd just had lunch.

"How can I help you?" Martha asked.

"Tara and I are talking to everyone who was at the meeting last night, trying to find out if anyone saw anything that could help explain what occurred. Paula asked to use the phone in the office shortly after we broke up. Did you happen to notice anyone heading in that direction?"

"I know folks were using the ladies' room. I remember seeing Alice, Stephanie, and Rachael heading in that direction at one time or another."

"Do you remember seeing everyone else in the main room?" I asked.

Martha didn't answer immediately. Finally, she said, "No. I'm sorry; I wasn't paying attention. I remember you were with Tara in the lounge and Paula going down the hallway. I thought she was going to use the ladies' room, but I guess she was going to use the phone. Rachael asked me about some books I was donating to the community yard sale and we got to chatting. Barbara and Alice joined us, and then Rachael excused herself to go to the ladies' room."

"Do you know for certain that's where Rachael went?"

Martha shook her head. "No. I didn't follow her, if that's what you mean. Surely you don't think Rachael...?"

"Not at this point," I reassured Martha. "Right now, we're just trying to map everyone's movements."

"I guess that makes sense. I wasn't moving around much myself, and because I had no idea what was going to happen I wasn't paying all that much attention to where everyone was during the break."

"Do you specifically remember where anyone else was between the time we decided to take the break and the time the lights went out?" I asked.

"I saw Jane chatting with Gwen, and it seems I remember seeing Sarah as well."

"Had you spoken to Paula at all other than as part of the group discussion?" Tara asked.

"No. I arrived at the store before she did and joined the others, and then I didn't speak to her after we broke."

"Do you happen to know if she was having any issues with any of the others?" Tara asked.

"No. It didn't seem like it to me. Everyone in the group seems to get along with everyone else just fine. One of the reasons I really love our little book club is because we all get along so well. I was in a book club that was held at the home of a woman I know from the library guild a few years back. The books that were selected were very good, but it seemed as if half the conversation centered on gossip and backstabbing rather than the books themselves. I quit after a while. It didn't seem worth it to go to all the trouble of reading the book and then not talk about it."

"That would be frustrating," I agreed.

I glanced at Tara, who picked up with the next question. "Had you heard that Paula and her husband had separated?"

"I'd heard rumors that she was having marital issues, but like I said, I'm not one to pay a lot of mind to rumors. A person's business is their business."

"I agree." Tara smiled.

"I just have one last question," I said. "Do you remember Paula mentioning anyone named Amber?"

Martha thought about it, then shook her head. "No. Seems I heard Henry has a niece with a similar name, though I'm pretty sure it's Amelia, not Amber. You can check with him just to be certain."

"I will," I answered. "Can you think of anything else you'd like to share?"

"Not really. Paula was a nice woman and she didn't deserve to be hurt that way. I hope you figure out who did it."

We left Martha's and headed to the Driftwood Café. Tara had gotten hold of Giselle on the phone. She'd said she was working that afternoon but things were slow and they had extra help, so she could take a break to speak to us. Giselle really was a beautiful woman. She had thick hair that hung down her back like a drape, although it was pinned up today. Her dark eyes seemed to sparkle with mystery when she spoke and her wide smiled welcomed you in. I guess I could see why Paula would feel threatened by her if she really did have cause to think Henry was interested in her.

"How can I help you?" Giselle asked after we'd scooted into a booth in the back.

"As I mentioned on the phone, Cait and I are talking to all the book club members, trying to figure out exactly what happened last night," Tara began.

"I'm still having a hard time believing it's all real. It seems impossible to believe that one of the women from book club killed Paula. There has to be another explanation."

"We hope so," Tara said. "But for now, the women who were at the meeting are all we have to go on. We're most interested in everyone's movements after we decided to take a break."

Giselle bowed her head. "I hate to admit it, but I slipped out for a smoke."

"But it was windy and there was lightning all around."

"I know, but when I get the craving it won't wait. I've tried to quit a bunch of times, but so far, the damn habit is winning the battle. Look, I know it seems crazy that I would go out in a storm to smoke, but that's exactly what I did. It was windy and the sky was filled with streaks of light, but it was barely raining by that point, so I plastered myself against the wall under the overhang. I came in when the lights inside went out. The sky opened up about ten seconds later. I didn't kill Paula, but I didn't see anything either."

I glanced at Tara, who shrugged.

"Did anyone come outside while you were smoking?" I asked.

"No. Not a single person. I don't think anyone else in the group smokes."

I decided to change things up a bit and asked Giselle about her impression of the sort of relationship Paula had with the others in the group.

"Look, I think I know where you're going with this," Giselle answered. "I spoke to Jane earlier. I know Paula accused me of having an affair with her husband. As if!" Giselle's face hardened. "I have plenty of men in my life. I certainly don't need to complicate things by messing around with a married man. I don't know where Paula got that idea, but it's absolutely not true." Giselle glanced at her watch. "I should get back. I really hope you figure out who did it, but it wasn't me."

"One thing before you go," I threw out. "Did Paula ever mention someone named Amber to you?"

Giselle narrowed her gaze. "No. Paula and I got along okay, but we weren't exactly friends. We rarely said a word to each other outside the book club discussion. If this Amber person is important you might ask Joy Holiday."

Joy owned a local toy store. "Joy and Paula were friends?"

"I'm not sure how close they were, but I've seen Joy and Paula meet here for lunch a few times. I think they're both part of the community theater group."

"Okay, I'll give her a call. Can you think of anyone else we should speak to?"

Giselle shrugged. "Not really. Paula was nice enough, but she was a little odd. I don't think she had a lot of friends outside of the ones she made in either the book club or the community theater group. I kind of felt bad for her. Although Joy made a point of spending time with her, she mentioned to me once that Paula was a lonely woman who wasn't all that close to her husband, had no children or other family she knew of, and never found her niche on the island."

"Thank you for sharing that, and for taking time to speak to us."

Tara and I went out to her car. "So what do you think?" she asked.

"On one hand Giselle doesn't have an alibi. She said she was outside alone and didn't speak to anyone during the time when Paula most likely was stabbed." I made a mark next to her name but didn't cross if off. "On the other hand it seemed like she was telling the truth. I guess we can ask the others if any of them saw Giselle either going out or coming back in after we lost power."

"That sounds like a good idea. Alice Jones texted me while we were chatting with Giselle," Tara informed me. "She gets off in an hour and we can come by her house in about ninety minutes if we want. In the meantime, I want to stop by The Bait and Stitch. I need some ribbon for Amy's costume."

Chapter 7

The Bait and Stitch is a unique shop owned by my Aunt Maggie and her best friend and business partner Marley Donnelly. It was created to blend Maggie's passion for fishing with Marley's passion for quilting. Both women loved to sew, so they'd allocated one room in the shop for a quilting room and, more often than not, the large circular table in it was occupied by the local gossips who made sure the residents of Madrona Island were informed with the latest news, be it fact or fiction.

When Tara and I arrived the hens were gathered to discuss the island's latest murder mystery.

"Oh Cait, I heard what happened." Maggie got up, crossed the room, and gave me a firm hug. "I'm so very sorry. How are you, dear?"

"I'm fine," I said as Maggie turned her attention to Tara, who also received a hug.

"Do they know who did it?" asked Doris Rutherford, the queen bee of the gossip group.

"Not yet," I responded. "Finn is working on it and the crime scene team from the county came by last night. Hopefully, we'll know something in a day or two."

"I understand everyone who was at the book club meeting is considered a suspect," Marley commented.

"I guess, to a degree. The back door to the store was locked from the inside and anyone coming or going through the front door would have been seen through the windows separating the seating area and cat lounge from the bookstore and coffee bar. I know it doesn't seem possible that one of the book club women could be guilty, but that's how it looks. Have any of you heard anything we should know?"

The women all looked among themselves. I had a feeling they knew something but were trying to decide whether they should tell us about it. I waited patiently, realizing it was a physical impossibility for the quilting gang not to spill the beans regarding even the smallest piece of gossip.

"You know I'm not one to gossip," Doris began. "But I have a friend who told me that she learned from a friend of a friend that Paula Wainwright and Rachael Steinway almost came to blows in the alley behind the bank a few days ago."

Rachael worked as an account manager at the bank, but I wasn't sure if she handled Paula's personal accounts. "Was Paula a customer of the bank?"

"I'm not really sure," Doris said, "but I know Paula temped there for two weeks when the girl who works the merchant window went on her honeymoon. If I had to guess I'd say Paula, the temporary employee, ruffled the feathers of Rachael, the account manager. Of course, I have no idea why, but I figured given what's happened you might want to know."

"I do want to know. Thank you for sharing. So far nothing we've learned is fitting together quite right, but you never know when a small detail could pull everything together."

"I figured you stopped by to pick our brains," Doris commented.

"Actually, we stopped by so Tara could buy some ribbon. The tip was just a happy bonus."

Marley popped up from her chair and turned to Tara. "What color ribbon can I help you find?"

"Black and orange. Amy is going to be a Halloween spider."

I joined the women at the table while Tara and Marley looked at ribbon samples. Much to Maggie's dismay, I had decided at a very early age that I hated to sew. Both Siobhan and Cassie shared my disdain for the activity and Maggie had never had daughters of her own, so she frequently complained that she didn't have anyone to share one of her favorite pastimes with.

"Will Cody be home in time for the Halloween Festival this weekend?" Maggie asked.

"He should be here on Friday. Hopefully, nothing will come up to keep him from arriving on time; we both volunteered to work the haunted house on Saturday."

"I haven't had a chance to check it out, but I hear it's the spookiest one yet," Doris said.

"There was even a protest by the preschool board that it wasn't as family-friendly as it once was," one of the other women commented. "Personally, I think if it's a haunted house it should be scary. The library is offering story time for the younger kids and the elementary school is hosting a kiddie carnival as well."

"It seems the island has activities for all age groups," I agreed. "St. Patrick's is hosting a chili feed on Saturday evening, the high school is having a dance on the thirty-first, and the senior center is holding a dance for adults of all ages, although the music's going to be ballroom, so I'm thinking it will be the over-fifty crowd that will attend."

"As far as I'm concerned, any dancing that isn't ballroom isn't really dancing," one of the women spoke up.

"What about ballet and tap?" another woman asked.

"Well, sure, *that's* dancing, but I was referring to the crazy moves the younger generation is in to. Most of it seems to consist of flaying your arms and legs around the room in a random fashion."

"I've seen some pretty amazing things on those talent shows," another woman countered.

"Did you catch *Dancing with the Stars* last week?" Doris said. "All I can say is, what were they thinking?"

I tried to listen, but I found myself tuning out. By the time the women at the table had finished discussing the merits of differing music and dancing styles, Tara had finished her shopping and we said our good-byes.

"What was that all about?" Tara asked as we headed to her car.

"Dancing. Are you and Parker planning to attend any of the dozen or so dances and parties being held in the area this weekend?"

"He's on call on Halloween, but we might go out on Saturday. I know there are several things going on in town. Maybe you and Cody should double date with us."

"That would be fun. We're working the haunted house until eight, but maybe we can meet you somewhere after."

"That would be perfect. We're taking Amy to the kiddie carnival at the school, but Parker mentioned getting a sitter so we could have some adult time too. I'll talk to him about it and let you know." Tara put her key in her car door and opened it. "So, on to Alice's place?"

"Yeah. It should be about time."

******

Alice Jones was married with two children and worked as a teacher's aide. She and her family lived in a small but charming home on the south end of

Harthaven. Alice was about the same age as we were, though unlike us, she hadn't grown up on the island. I didn't know her well, but I did enjoy the time we spent together at book club. She was a very sweet and seemingly caring individual who I thought spread happiness wherever she went.

"Perfect timing," Alice said as she greeted us at the front door. "Timmy and Tammy are down for their naps, so we should be able to chat without interruption. Can I get you some iced tea? I'm afraid all I have is plain. My husband finished off the sweet tea when he came home for lunch. I have sugar, so you can add it to the plain tea if you'd like."

"Plain is fine," I said.

Tara agreed and we followed Alice into the small kitchen.

"Have a seat at the table. You can just shove the crayons aside."

Tara gathered up the discarded coloring sticks while I stacked the coloring books into a pile. We set everything on one end of the table and then sat down at the other.

"First, I want to say how very sorry I am about Paula," Alice said as she set large glasses of iced tea in front of us. "I was so upset when I heard. Who would do such a horrible thing?"

"That's what we're trying to figure out," I answered. "We're speaking to everyone who was at book club last night so we can put together a map of sorts."

"Of course. It makes sense to figure out who was with whom and who might have seen the killer enter the hallway. How can I help?"

I rested my arms on the table and made eye contact with Alice before asking my first question. "Do you remember what you did and who you saw or talked to after we decided to take that break?"

Alice took a minute to consider. "I had to use the ladies' room, so I headed there first. There was already someone inside and Barbara was in line, so I got behind her. Stephanie got behind me and we talked about the book for a minute."

"Do you remember seeing Paula?"

"Yes. She was going into your office just as I was coming out of the ladies' room. She was alone and seemed to have something on her mind. I didn't speak to her. After I went back to the group I spoke with Martha and Barbara until the lights went out and everyone began to panic."

I sat forward slightly. "You said Stephanie was in line behind you. Was anyone else in line by the time you came out of the ladies' room?"

"I didn't see anyone. I do kind of remember Rachael heading in that direction after I went back into the main room. It was such an odd sort of evening. We'd been discussing a spooky book and Tara had done such a good job with the decorations that the room had a spooky feel. And there was all that thunder and lightning and the wind was about as bad as I've ever seen it. I remember thinking there was a feeling of electricity in the room, almost as if my senses were buzzing. When the lights went out I began to panic. It was a good thing Martha was nearby to steady me."

"Can you think of anything that occurred last night that could be relevant? Was someone acting odd or did any of the women in the building seem to be bickering?"

Alice shook her head. "No. Everyone seemed perfectly normal. I guess maybe it was a little odd that Gwen joined our group when the lights went out instead of making sure Sarah was okay. The two sisters seem to be so close, more like good friends."

"Do you know where Sarah was?" Tara asked.

"I didn't see her. Of course, it was dark and everyone was scared. When we all huddled together Barbara started praying so loud it hurt my ears. Looking back, I suppose we all should have been praying. It was a pretty serious situation, being out there on the wharf, with the waves crashing against the pilings while the wind blew so hard it felt like the building was going to blow down, and the lightning was right on top of our heads. I don't know if I've ever been that scared."

"Do you remember if you saw Giselle at any point after we called for the break?" I asked.

Alice thought about it, then shook her head. "I don't specifically remember seeing her. I'm sure she must have been there, though. We all were."

"Except for Paula."

"Yeah, I guess it is odd that I didn't realize she wasn't with us."

"It was a confusing and rather nerve-racking time," Tara comforted her. "Everyone we've spoken to so far has mentioned the fact that they hadn't realized Paula was missing and only specifically remembered seeing a few others they could identify."

Alice bent and unbent the corner of a napkin in what looked to be a nervous gesture. "I guess that makes me feel better, but I still feel bad I didn't notice Paula's absence. Maybe we could have helped her if we'd realized she wasn't with us."

"Yeah, maybe," I agreed. "Do you know if Paula had a problem or argument with anyone in the group?"

Alice shook her head. "Not that she or anyone else ever mentioned to me. We weren't close friends and only spoke during the book discussions. She seemed like she got along all right with the others as far as I could tell."

"Did Paula ever mention anyone named Amber to you?"

Alice frowned. "I don't think so. Is someone named Amber involved in this?"

"We aren't sure. It's just a name that came up."

We spoke to Alice for a while longer, then headed out to Tara's car. She had a date to have dinner with Parker and Amy that evening and was going to drop me off, then go home to get ready. I had choir practice and then planned to head home to get a good night's rest. I missed Cody when he was away, but I was especially feeling his absence with a murder mystery to solve and a choir to lead by myself.

"I think we can eliminate Martha, Alice, Jane, and Barbara from our suspect list," I said as Tara drove. "They all seemed to have been with someone who had since corroborated that fact."

"I agree, except for Jane. She said she chatted with Gwen, so I'd like to speak to her before we eliminate her from the list."

"I might stop by to speak to Gwen after choir practice. She's in class during the day, so it would be easier to catch her in the evening."

"If you want to do that we'll try to track down Sarah, Rachael, and Stephanie tomorrow. We might want to speak to Joy as well. Maybe by this time tomorrow we'll have things figured out."

I really hoped so, though my gut told me it wasn't going to be that easy.

Chapter 8

When I arrived home Cassie called and asked me if I wanted to grab some dinner with her. I loved my little sister and was happy to spend time with her, but she's a senior in high school with a slew of friends of her own, so I wondered why she wanted to spend time with me. Until recently, she hadn't given me the time of day unless she needed me to run interference with our mom, but we'd bonded over the summer, when a girl her age had come to Madrona Island to visit Cody and the four of us had gotten mixed up in a complicated murder investigation.

I did have choir practice and I wanted to meet with Gwen, who'd said she could meet whenever, so I figured I'd see her before choir and then arrange to meet

Cassie afterward. It would be a late dinner, but Cassie didn't seem to mind.

Gwen was a fifty-three-year-old widow who taught math at the high school and lived just down the street from her sister Sarah, also a widow. She was waiting for me when I arrived. She showed me in and offered me a beverage, which I declined. I explained that I had to get to choir practice and didn't have a lot of time. I also mentioned I planned to have dinner with Cassie after choir and Gwen expressed her opinion that my sister had blossomed this year after almost flunking out of math as a sophomore. She wondered if Cassie had finally begun to grow into the woman we all knew she was capable of becoming.

"Cassie seemed to turn a corner when our family home burned down and our mother and I almost died in the blaze," I explained. "I think she realized life is fragile and doesn't come with any sort of guarantee. It was as if she matured overnight. She's doing well in school now, helping out at the church, getting along with Mom, and generally has become a pleasant person to be around."

"I'm so very happy to hear that."

"The main reason I'm here," I went on, "is to ask you about your memory of what occurred last night before everyone left."

"I'm happy to help if I can. I can't believe poor Paula is dead. It seems almost surreal when I consider that she was murdered while we were all in the next room and no one says they heard anything. If someone attacked me in the dark I'd be screaming like a banshee."

"The storeroom is somewhat removed from the room where the group meets and there was a lot of noise from the wind and thunder, but I agree, it does seem someone should have heard something."

"I suppose she could have frozen when she realized someone was in the room with her. I spoke to Jane, who told me the whole thing happened at about the time the lights went out."

I nodded. "Yes, it was about then. When we decided to take the break Paula asked to use the phone in the office. That's the last anyone seems to have seen of her. Do you remember seeing her at all after that point?"

"No, I'm afraid I didn't see a thing."

"Can you tell me exactly what you did and who you spoke to after we broke?"

Gwen adjusted her position before she began speaking. She appeared to be uncomfortable. Not that I blamed her; this was an uncomfortable situation. "After the break was called I spoke to Sarah for a while. We saw Paula walk by, and she told me she wanted to ask Paula a question about the accounting firm she works for. I saw Jane coming from the ladies' room and I chatted with her until the lights went out and we all gathered in the cat lounge."

"Okay; who do you remember seeing in the cat lounge?"

"I remember Alice, Barbara, Jane, and Martha being there. I know there were others, but it was dark and we were all crammed in together."

"Do you specifically remember seeing Sarah?"

"Not at first. She did mention needing to use the ladies' room too, so she may have stopped off there after speaking to Paula. I did see Sarah later, after things began to calm down a bit."

"Do you know what Sarah wanted to speak to Paula about?" I asked.

"Not specifically," Gwen answered. "You know Sarah works for an accounting firm in Harthaven, and Paula had been subbing for an accounting firm in Pelican Bay. It seemed to me there was a customer who was transferring between one firm and the other. I'm not sure which firm he was leaving and which he was changing to, but it seemed there was a question or issue Sarah thought Paula could help her with."

"I know Paula's husband is an accountant. Was that the firm Paula was subbing for?"

"No. It was a different one. Henry works for Calvin and Coleman. Paula was subbing for a small company, with only one accountant."

It sounded as if Gwen had an alibi but Sarah, not so much. I really hoped she wouldn't end up being the killer. I stayed on for a few minutes with Gwen, but she didn't seem to know much more, so I asked her about Amber before I left.

"No," Gwen shook her head, "I don't remember Paula mentioning an Amber. There are several Ambers at the high school, but I can't imagine she was involved with any of them. Could it be someone she knew before moving to the island?"

"Probably," I answered. "I'm not sure if the name is relevant, but it seemed it might be a clue, so I'm asking everyone about it. If you think of something that might help us figure out who killed Paula, please give me a call."

"I will, dear. And have fun dining with your sister."

I headed to church and choir practice. I was alone tonight without so much as a pianist, so I asked Sister Mary if she'd be willing to help. She was happy to. When rehearsal was over and the kids had all left I took the opportunity to ask her about her meetings with Tara.

"I'm happy she feels comfortable enough to ask me the things she has on her mind," Sister Mary said. "I've had a lot of years to reconcile the fact that I was born Maryellen Thornton, into a wealthy but cold family, and that I lived for more than a decade as Jane Farmington, wife of Jim Farmington, the man who killed my parents and kidnapped and raped me. I've made peace with the fact that I gave my baby daughter away to protect her and fled to a convent, where I became Sister Mary. It hasn't always been easy to keep the various phases of my life compartmentalized but somehow, with God's help, I've done it. Poor Tara hasn't had time to process everything. She doesn't even seem to know what it is she wants and needs to understand. I think in the beginning acceptance of the situation was easier than it is now. I'm not sure how much our talks are helping, but I do what I can. All I want for her—all I've ever wanted for her—was to be happy and have a normal life."

I put my hand on Sister Mary's. "I know that and I think she does as well. My take on things is that her emotional distress has more to do with the fact that her father was a monster than anything else. I know she loves you. She loved you before she knew you were her mother. And I know she respects that you've been able to move on with your life, leaving all the ugliness behind. I have a feeling she'll be okay in the long run. She has a wonderful support system and a woman she admires to help her along the way."

Sister Mary's eyes were filled with concern. "I hope you're right."

"I've known Tara my whole life. She's strong and she's a fighter. She'll figure things out." I glanced at the clock on the wall. "I'm meeting Cassie for dinner. Thanks for helping with choir practice. I really appreciate it."

"Of course, dear. Thank you for all you do for the church and the families who attend."

I arrived at Antonio's to find Cassie already there at a table. She was sipping a soda and I ordered myself a glass of wine. We both chose spaghetti and meatballs for dinner and once our order was placed, I asked how she'd been and what she'd been up to.

"I've been good. I'm doing better in school and have even decided to go to college, which is what I wanted to talk to you about."

"That's wonderful." I grinned. "But if you want to know about colleges you should talk to Siobhan. She's your only sibling who went."

"I don't need advice about colleges, at least not yet. What I wanted to talk about is Mom."

"Mom?"

"If I go away to college she'll be alone. That worries me."

I took a minute to consider that. "You *are* the last child left at home, but Mom has four other children living on the island. It's not like she'll be alone."

"I know that, but now that Aiden has his own place, if I go away to school she'll be living alone. When I mentioned college to her she hugged me and said she was proud of me, but I could see that she was sad. She's never lived alone before."

Cassie had a point. Mom probably would be sad when Cassie went away to school, but things had changed in the past year. She no longer lived in the huge Hart home where we all grew up, and she had

Gabe, a man she'd met recently but had been dating steadily.

"I think it's awesome that you're concerned about Mom, but I think she'll be fine. It seems like her relationship with Gabe is progressing. I'm willing to bet she most likely won't be living alone for long."

"You really think they'll get married?" Cassie asked.

"I don't know for sure, but it seems like that's the direction they're headed. I realize Gabe needs to be sensitive to his daughter's feelings now that he's moved on after the death of his wife, but Mom has told me she's prepared to wait. But I do think they're working toward something permanent. Why don't you talk to her about your concerns if you're feeling uncertain?"

Cassie didn't answer, and I could see she was unsure about doing that.

"So, what are you thinking of majoring in?" I asked after a moment.

"You're never going to believe it, but I'm thinking of mathematics. I know it wasn't all that long ago that I was flunking out and insisted math was dumb and I'd never be able to figure it out, but once I started to understand how things fit together I realized it was kind of cool. I spoke to Ms. Peterman and she told me some of the professions you can go into with a degree in mathematics. I had no idea there were so many."

I placed my hand over Cassie's. "That's really wonderful. I'm happy you found something you're passionate about. I know Mom will be happy as well. Talk to her. Tell her how you're feeling. I imagine it might take some time for her to get used to the idea, but in the end I'm sure she'll be thrilled with your decision. And she does have the rest of us to rely on. I'll make more of an effort to spend time with her once you're gone and I know Siobhan will as well. And you'll be home for holidays and summer break."

"That's true. I guess I feel better. Thanks, Cait."

We paused the conversation as our salads and garlic bread arrived. Once we'd begun eating our entrées I brought up Cassie's new friend who'd visited over the summer. I knew they kept in touch via email.

"Have you heard from Alyson?"

"Yeah. We chat every week. She's doing great and is loving being a senior as much as I am. She told me that she's involved in a haunted house thing this weekend with her friends. It sounded totally cool. I wish I could have gone for a visit, but I had too much homework to get caught up on."

"I hear the haunted house on the island is going to be scary this year. Maybe you and some of your friends can try it."

"I'm going on Friday night with this guy I've been seeing. His name is Jeremy and he's really nice. Mom even likes him."

"I didn't know you had a new boyfriend. I'd like to meet him."

"Maybe we can meet up at some point over the weekend. Jeremy's into math like I am, although he's into applied math. I think he wants to be an engineer, whereas I love the theoretical stuff." Cassie, who was looking toward the door, waved at someone. "Oh look; Danny's here."

The younger of my two brothers walked over and kissed Cassie on the cheek. "Hey, stranger," he greeted her. "I haven't seen you in a month."

"Been busy. Do you want to join us?"

"Thanks, but I'm meeting someone. I'll catch you both later."

I watched Cassie, whose eyes were on Danny as he walked away. She turned and looked at me. "Isn't he still dating that girl he introduced us to a few months ago? It seemed like they were serious."

A woman I'd never met walked in and kissed Danny on the lips. "Apparently not."

"Why is it the men in our family can't seem to settle down? Aiden has never had a really serious relationship and he's thirty-five, and Danny seems to have a new relationship every time I see him. Siobhan is married and you have Cody. I'm only seventeen, but I've had longer-term relationships than either of our brothers."

I shrugged. "I guess it's just a guy thing."

"I guess, but I worry about the fact that Aiden and Danny will end up old men with no families."

I chuckled. "You actually think about stuff like that?" As far as I could tell, Cassie's thoughts usually didn't run deeper than the hot new guy in her life and the newest color nail polish. I guess she really was growing up.

"I'll admit I didn't used to think about the love life of my siblings or how it would affect their future, but things have been different since the fire. I feel like life is passing them by, especially Aiden. He's almost as old as some of my friends' parents. In fact, I have one friend whose parents are thirty-six. When Aiden lived at home with Mom and me I never thought about him being lonely, but now that he has his own place I do wonder if he's happy or lonely."

"I'm sure if Aiden is lonely there are plenty of women on the island who would be happy to date him."

Cassie shrugged. "I guess. I hope he finds someone. Danny too. I want my kids to grow up in a big family with lots of cousins, and so far, the only one who's really on the ball is Siobhan."

"I hope you won't have kids for a while, and by then everything could have changed."

"I hope so. Should we order dessert?"

"I'm stuffed, but you go ahead. Dinner's my treat."

Cassie grinned and ordered a piece of Oreo cake and a glass of chocolate milk to wash it down. One minute she was a young woman worrying about her future and the futures of the rest of the family and the next she was a kid with a chocolate milk mustache, licking the frosting off her cake.

Chapter 9

Thursday, October 26

Tara had set up interviews with Rachael Steinway and Sarah Frost for later that day. Both women had jobs, so we had to work the meetings around their schedules. Although Sarah could get away from the accounting firm she worked for in Harthaven for a half hour at around eleven, Rachael wouldn't have free time from the bank until around two. Tara had paperwork she wanted to get done in the morning, so I headed over to the toy store to speak with Joy Holiday and then would meet Tara in time to see Sarah.

While the toy store was packed during both the summer and weekends and between Thanksgiving and Christmas, it was pretty dead on weekdays in October. Joy had done a fantastic job of decorating the place to look like Dracula's castle, with all sorts of Halloween accents to bring people in off the street. I couldn't remember there being a toy store that went to so much trouble to ignite the imagination when I was growing up, and I found I enjoyed spending time in this magical place that changed its décor with the seasons.

"I love your decorations," I said as soon as I walked in the door.

"Thank you." Joy smiled. "I spent a lot of time putting everything up, but I think it was worth it. Halloween is my favorite holiday, although I make most of my profit at Christmas, so I guess I love that one as well."

I picked up a mechanical Frankenstein and watched as it moved its arms and legs in a stiff way. It was cute. In the world of today's technology, it was a bit retro but cute. "I stopped by to ask you about Paula Wainwright. I understand you were friends."

"Sort of. I met her when she first came to the island. We got to talking and realized we had a lot in common in terms of literature and music. She was interested in the community theater and I was as well. I wouldn't say we were best friends, but she seemed kind of lonely, so I made a point of spending time with her. We went to lunch a couple of times a month and occasionally went to dinner when we were both in a play and had rehearsals."

"I understand Barbara Jenkins also participates in community theater."

"Yes, she does. The three of us would all go to dinner sometimes. I can't believe Paula's dead. It seems so senseless." Joy led me over to a small table with coloring books on it and motioned for me to sit down. "I want to help in any way I can. What can I tell you?"

"Honestly, I'm not sure. I've been speaking to all the women who were at book club that night and so far, I can't identify a single reason anyone would want to kill Paula. A couple of the women have said she'd seemed depressed and distracted lately. I don't know if it's relevant to her death, but I wondered what had been going on in her life."

Joy paused before answering. "Paula spent a lifetime dealing with depression. I don't think it was an everyday occurrence, but since I've known her it seems her overall mood and mental health seemed to cycle between normal behavior and extreme depression. When she had her depression under control she was happy, focused, and generous. During those times she got along well with everyone. But when a depression cycle set in, she became secretive and paranoid. In the three years I knew her, I witnessed two depression cycles. It seemed to me that extreme and somewhat erratic behavior seemed to be a prelude to the depression, and based on what I witnessed in the past couple of weeks, I believe she may have been entering another depression phase."

"So her depression and paranoia were the result of a chemical imbalance?"

"I believe so, although I'm not really qualified to make such a statement. I asked her once why she didn't seek treatment. I understand a steady dose of the right drug can really help people like Paula, but she told me she'd tried medication and the meds made her feel strange, so she stopped taking them. She told me she didn't mind the low times in her life. I know it seems odd, but she said she felt more herself during the depression cycles."

"That does seem odd."

"I think Paula had a tragic past. She didn't tell me exactly what happened, but I got the impression she felt the need to offer penance. When she was down and miserable she felt she was doing that, but when she was happy and healthy she felt she didn't deserve the good things she had."

"From what I understand, Paula had kicked her husband out of the house on several occasions. Do you think she felt she didn't deserve him, so she was sabotaging their relationship?"

"Perhaps. I don't know this for certain, but it did seem her paranoia about Henry cheating began around the same time I noticed her overall mood change. Of course, if Henry really was cheating, that alone could account for a melancholy mood. I'm not a mental health professional and certainly don't claim to know how depression works; I can only report what I saw during the three years I knew her."

"I know Paula had been working for a temp agency. Did she need the job or was she just trying to fill her time?"

Joy shrugged. "I'm not sure. It seemed Henry made good money, but I'm inclined to believe he may have limited his financial support after she kicked him out. Paula seemed to enjoy the temp work at first. It allowed her to change jobs every couple of weeks, which I think suited her."

"You said *at first*. Did something change?"

"It seemed like it. I guess it was about a month ago that her dark mood began to show through. She was working for a law firm at the time and I have a feeling she learned something that bothered her. She never did say what it was, but she began acting secretive and paranoid. It could simply have been the depression setting in. I'm really not sure."

"Do you know where she worked after the law firm?"

"The bank, but I don't think that worked out. By the time the bank job came to an end she was in a pretty low place and didn't take another assignment."

"Did Paula kick Henry out before or after the job at the law firm?"

"Before. I'm pretty sure it was the problem between them that caused her to take the temp job in the first place. Although..."

"Although what?" I asked.

Joy frowned. "I'm not sure exactly. It sort of seemed like the job with the temp agency was a bit more intentional that her simply needing a job and taking the first thing that came along. I can't know what her thought process was, but it did seem to start with Henry."

"Did Paula ever tell you who she thought Henry was having an affair with?"

"No, not specifically. But she did mention in passing that she needed to find Amber and was thinking of hiring a private investigator to do it. I asked her who Amber was and she looked startled, like she hadn't been aware she'd even said the name aloud. She told me Amber was no one, that she was just talking to herself. A week after that she told me she'd kicked out Henry because she'd found proof he was cheating, and it made me wonder."

"So you think Paula hired a PI to track down Amber to prove she was cheating with Henry?"

"That was my take on things, but as I said before, I really don't know for certain."

I decided not to mention the note with the name Amber on it, but I was curious about the dates. "Do April 12, 1999, or November 6, 2014, mean anything to you?"

"No, although November 6, 2014, would be about the time I first met Paula. I wouldn't say it was that exact date, but it was just before Thanksgiving three years ago and she'd just come here, so I suppose it could be the day she moved to Madrona."

If that were true—and I had no way to know if it was—maybe the date in 1999 was the one when something began and the date she moved here was the one when it ended. Seemed like a long shot, but at this point I didn't have much to go on.

I left the toy store and headed home. It was a little early to pick up Tara and I knew she had something she wanted to finish before we started off for the day, so I figured I'd take Max for a quick run on the beach just in case I ended up getting home late again. When I opened the cabin door Frank ran out before I could catch him.

"Geez. If you want to go for a walk with Max and me you just need to ask. I almost tripped over you."

"Meow." Frank trotted over to the car and started scratching at the door.

"You want to go somewhere?"

"Meow."

I looked back toward the cabin. "Okay, but let's take Max. The poor guy has been getting left alone a lot lately." I went into the cabin and Frank followed me. "Any idea where it is we're going?" I asked.

Frank jumped onto the counter where I had left a variety of items I needed to sort through. Most of it was junk, but I didn't want to start throwing stuff away without making sure I wasn't getting rid of something I might need. One of the items on the counter was a flyer Tara had printed a couple of weeks earlier inviting people to the book club meeting the previous Tuesday. Frank selected it and pushed it onto the floor.

"Book club?" I asked.

"Meow."

"You want to go somewhere related to Paula's death? The bookstore?"

Frank just looked at me.

"No, I guess it isn't that. Paula's house?"

"Meow." Frank ran to the door and waited for me to open it.

I turned and looked at Max. "Apparently, we're going for a ride. Want to come?"

Max went to the door as well, so I loaded both animals into the car and headed back to Paula's house, where I'd made book deliveries a time or two. Of course, I had no idea how I'd get inside if the door was locked, which I imagine it was, but I figured if Frank was running the show he could figure out what to do when we got there.

I parked down the street just a bit so as not to call attention to the fact that I was checking out the house. Then I followed Frank and Max followed me as we headed down the sidewalk and around to the back of the house. I didn't see anyone in the area, so I hoped no one would call the cops to report a break-in. I probably should have told Finn what I was doing, though he'd only tell me not to enter Paula's house, and I knew it was important to follow Frank wherever he took me.

Frank led Max and me to the cement steps that led down to a cellar. When he got to the door he paused, so I opened it and he went inside, with us behind him. On the far side of the unfinished room were wooden stairs leading up. They led to another door, also not locked, which opened into a long, narrow hallway. Frank trotted to a door at the end of the hall. It seemed as if he knew exactly where he was going. I opened the door, which led into a master suite. The bed was unmade, the dresser littered with various items that, based on the layer of dust, must have been there for quite some time.

Frank went directly to a small desk that held a phone, a laptop computer, and a notebook. He jumped up onto the desktop and pushed the notebook to the floor. I opened it and found handwritten notes I assumed were made by Paula. There were dates, phone numbers, addresses, and even a shopping list. I assumed she used the notebook as some sort of calendar. I slipped the notebook into my backpack and looked at the cat. "Anything else?"

His answer was to trot down the hall to the wooden stairway.

"Okay, it seems I have what we came for, but give me a minute to look around." I walked down the hallway, opening and closing doors. It looked as if most of the rooms hadn't been touched in some time. They were probably guest rooms I suspected Paula only went into when she had guests to fill them. I did notice, though, that there were men's clothing in the closet of one and wondered if Henry hadn't had his own room before he moved out. Of course, if he'd had his own room he wouldn't have known about Paula's late-night calls—which reminded me that I needed to follow up with Finn about that.

The living area was dusty and cluttered with unopened mail, alcohol bottles, and empty glasses. I guess if Paula had been feeling depressed she hadn't bothered with cleaning. The kitchen revealed a few dirty plates but mostly empty glasses and an ashtray full of cigarette butts. Odd; I'd never seen Paula smoke. I had to wonder if someone else had been spending time in the house. I opened the refrigerator and found the only food inside was well past its use-by date.

I thought back to the last couple of book club meetings. Now that I thought about it, I guess it had looked as if Paula had lost weight, but she hadn't appeared to be drinking. At least not on the nights she joined the group. She had, however, missed the meeting before last, so I hadn't seen her for two months before this week.

Once I'd assuaged my curiosity I indicated to Frank that I was ready to go, and Max and I followed him back down the stairs into the cellar, then back out into the yard and to the car. I didn't have time to study the notebook before meeting Tara, so I dropped the animals back at the cabin and drove to Tara's condo.

******

"Oh good, you're here," Tara greeted me. "Sarah called to say her schedule has changed a bit and she wants us to come earlier."

"I'm ready when you are."

"We'll take my car," Tara offered. "Less cat hair."

Tara was right. She had one cat, Bandit, who occasionally went places with her but not on a regular basis, whereas I had Max as well as multiple cats in my car almost every day. I tried to keep it vacuumed, but in the end, it was a losing proposition.

Sarah had arranged for us to meet in the conference room of the accounting firm for which she worked. She was waiting there for us when the receptionist showed us in.

"I'm sorry I had to move this up, but I have a client coming in at eleven-thirty."

"No problem. We can be quick," I said. "I guess Tara told you that we're speaking to everyone who was at the bookstore on the night Paula died."

"Yes. And I want to help in any way I can."

"We're attempting to map everyone's movements that night," I added.

Sarah was silent for a moment. "You think one of us killed her?"

"I don't want to believe that, but we were in a locked building, so it seems likely that one of the club members is the killer. I really hope a new theory will come to light."

"Have you considered that there was already someone inside the store before the book club members arrived?"

I glanced at Tara, who had a contemplative look on her face.

"So, you're suggesting someone came in during the store's regular operating hours and hid out inside until the evening?"

"I guess I'm just saying that could be a possibility. All I'm trying to do is offer another explanation that would explain how Paula could have been murdered without the killer being one of us."

"You've made a good point and we'll definitely look at that option. In the meantime, can you tell us what you did and who you spoke to after we decided to take a break?"

Sarah nodded. "I can try. Let's see. I chatted with Gwen for a few minutes and then I saw Paula heading to the office. I needed to speak to her about a customer who was transferring from the accounting firm she'd been subbing for to this one. I wrapped up my conversation with Gwen and followed Paula. When I got there I could hear Paula on the phone, so I decided to use the ladies' room. When I came out the storm seemed to be intensifying, so I went back to the main room of the bookstore."

I took a minute to process what she'd said. We already knew Jane, Barbara, Alice, and Stephanie had also gone to the ladies' room. Alice had reported that she'd seen Paula going into the office as she was coming out of the restroom. If Stephanie had been quick and Sarah hadn't immediately followed Paula, as she'd indicated she hadn't, the ladies' room could have been empty by the time Sarah walked down the hall.

"Do you remember seeing Giselle during the break?" I asked.

"No, I don't, though in all fairness, I wasn't taking a head count, so I don't specifically remember seeing a lot of us."

"Had you ever heard Paula mention someone named Amber?"

"No. Why?"

"Her name just came up. We aren't sure it means anything. Was there anyone you definitely saw and can vouch for?"

"Gwen, of course, and I saw Jane talking to Gwen as well. I remember seeing Stephanie and Martha. Oh, and Barbara. I wish I could be more helpful, but with the storm and all, it seemed like things happened really quickly."

Sarah's customer arrived, so Tara and I said our good-byes. We still had more than two hours before we could meet with Rachael, so we headed out to my cabin to have a bite to eat there and look through the notebook Frank had led me to earlier in the morning.

Chapter 10

"Okay, this is strange," Tara said as we ate tuna sandwiches and studied the notebook. So far, it looked like Paula had, as I'd thought, used it to jot down notes and things she needed to remember, like phone numbers, appointments, and grocery lists.

"What's strange?" I asked as I nibbled on a potato chip.

"This page is set up like a ledger. See this first column of numbers? I could be wrong, but to me they look like bank account numbers, and the second column has dollar amounts, so that fits. The third column is a bit different, but I'd say they're customer numbers." Tara glanced up from the page she was looking at. "I have no idea if this is in any way related to Paula's death, but I think it could be."

I frowned. "I suppose. Money does seem to be at the root of a lot of murders. I wonder if those are her accounts or the account information of someone else."

"I'm not sure, but the dollar amounts are big. Paula didn't appear to have a lot of money. If she did I don't know why she would be messing around with all the temp jobs she'd been taking. I wonder if we can find out whether these really are account numbers and who they belong to."

"We're meeting with Rachael this afternoon and she works at the same bank where Paula was temping. Maybe she can tell us what we're looking at."

Tara tore out the page and handed it to me. "Let's bring this with us and we can ask her. I didn't find anything else interesting, although we might want to find out who this phone number belongs to." Tara pointed to a number jotted down on another page. "I imagine Finn has pulled Paula's phone records by now, so we can ask him."

"I'll call him after I finish eating. You said there were several phone numbers in the notebook. Why are you focusing on that particular one?"

"It looks like she came back to it several times." Tara pushed the book toward me. "See how there are all these doodles? And there are doodles surrounding most of the numbers I found, which indicates to me that Paula liked to doodle while she talked on the phone. But this number has a lot of doodles, and many of them were done in different-colored ink. I'm not sure it's significant, but it seems to indicate it's a number she called many times."

I studied the page Tara had shoved in front of me. There were doodles in black, blue, and even red ink. "Okay. I'll see if Finn knows whose number it is. Anything else?"

"Without more to go on, not really. I'm not sure there's anything in the notebook. We may just be grasping at anything we can find."

I glanced at Frank, who was curled up on a chaise longue. "There has to be something relevant in this notebook. Frank wouldn't have gone to all the trouble of taking me to fetch it if there wasn't. Whether we're on the right track with the account numbers and phone number I don't know, but I'm quite certain something in this book is going to provide us with the clue we need."

"I've been thinking about what Sarah said about the killer already being on the premises. Although it seems unlikely, it's possible. People are in and out of the store all day long. It would be entirely possible for someone to sneak in and hide in the storeroom."

"Maybe," I answered. "But something doesn't feel right. For one thing, the use of our box-opening knife as a murder weapons seems random. More like a weapon of opportunity. If someone snuck in and hid in the storage room waiting for the opportunity to kill Paula why not bring a weapon with them? They couldn't have known the knife would be just sitting there."

"True," Tara acknowledged. "And they couldn't have known Paula would use the phone, which would put her near the storeroom. It *is* all very random."

I paused, then said, "Paula said she needed to make a call. Maybe the killer contacted her with either a call or a text and asked her to call them right away. That could provide a way to get Paula into the office."

Tara shook her head. "No, I don't think so. The killer would have to have known ahead of time that Paula's cell battery would be dead and that we'd take a break. I think you were right the first time. It's all too random."

"Unless someone was in the storeroom for another reason and Paula's murder was a wrong-place-at-the-wrong-time sort of thing."

"What do you mean, another reason? What other reason?"

"For the sake of this discussion, let's say someone snuck into the storage room earlier in the day for some random reason. Maybe to steal something or to find a place to sleep where they knew they'd be able to avoid being caught in the storm. What if they were moving around in the storeroom and Paula heard them after she made her call? She went into the room to check it out and the killer panicked and thrust a knife in her chest."

"Okay, then where did they go afterward?"

"They snuck out when we were all huddled in the cat lounge during the worst of the storm. Between the electrical failure and the sheer panic everyone was feeling, it's totally conceivable that no one would have noticed someone sneaking out."

"Maybe, but if I was the killer I would have gone out the back door, and we both know it was locked from the inside. And I think I would have taken the knife with me so the sheriff's office couldn't pull prints or other evidence from it. I know we both want the killer to be someone other than a book club member, but in the end, I think it's going to be one of them."

"Yeah, I guess you're right. It would make things a lot easier if it did turn out to be a random person taking refuge from the storm, though." I glanced out at the dark clouds on the horizon. The air and sea were both calm, but I had a feeling things were going to change by the end of the afternoon. "I'm finished with my lunch. I'll call Finn to see what he has to say."

Before I made the call I took my plate into the cabin and gave Max the leftover tuna, which wasn't enough to keep for another time. Then I grabbed a sweatshirt because the wind was beginning to pick up and headed out onto the deck, where Tara was sitting with Frank. I dialed Finn's cell and waited.

"Hey, Cait. What's up?"

"I'm just checking in. We've completed all but two interviews and I wanted to compare notes before we headed out for the afternoon. I also wanted to ask you about a phone number we found in a notebook that was Paula's."

"Do I want to know how you happened to come into possession of that notebook?" Finn asked.

"Probably not," I said, then read him the number.

"That's the number Paula called from your office on the night she died. The one that led to the burner phone."

"And you never found out who it belonged to?"

"Not so far. I've been calling it periodically, but no one has answered. I've been trying to track the purchase location by the product number. It looks like it was bought out of state. There are only three chains that carry this brand in Washington. I checked with them and found the model attached to the number is only available east of the Rockies."

"Why would different models be available in different areas?"

"It's a marketing ploy. It's possible a third-party retailer sold the phone on the internet, so I'm not sure we'll be able to narrow this down. I'm still working on it, though, just in case I catch a break."

"As long as we're talking about phone numbers, did you ever figure out who was calling Paula in the middle of the night?"

"I only found two calls to her house line between midnight and six a.m. Both were made from Paula's cell phone to her landline."

"Why on earth would Paula call her home phone in the middle of the night?"

"I have no idea. Maybe she was messing with Henry."

"Wouldn't he have seen her making the call?"

"Not if he was asleep and she made the call from bed. The landline ringing would have woken him up, but if it was on Paula's side of the bed and she answered it, he never would have known she was the one to make the call in the first place."

"This is becoming more and more bizarre."

"Tell me about it. Most of what we've found so far makes no sense at all."

"Did you find any prints on the knife?"

"There were prints from three different people: you, Tara, and Paula."

"Paula?"

"She may have grabbed the knife and tried to pull it out before she lost consciousness."

"Okay, that makes sense, but are you sure there aren't any other prints that could belong to the killer?"

"Not unless you or Tara did it."

"Ha, ha; very funny." I paused to let everything sink in. "The killer must have worn gloves."

"It would seem to be the case, but a killer wearing gloves doesn't fit the rest of the setup. The use of a knife sitting on a nearby table seems to indicate a killing of opportunity, whereas gloves make it seem intentional."

I frowned and glanced at Tara. I could see she was curious about the details of our conversation. "One of the women we spoke to suggested that the killer might already have been in the storeroom before the book club even started. Tara and I have discussed that possibility and feel it's conceivable someone could have snuck in to find a place to ride out the storm they were aware was coming and maybe Paula heard them moving around and went to investigate and got herself stabbed for her trouble."

"Then where were they when you and Tara went in to look for Paula?"

I explained about the dark room and overall chaos and the theory that the killer snuck out. "Though it doesn't fit that a homeless person taking refuge would be wearing gloves. Actually, the whole idea of anyone wearing gloves doesn't fit. It was stormy but not cold enough to warrant digging out the winter gloves. If the killer used gloves they would have to have had the gloves on them at the time they confronted Paula. And the only scenario where that works is if Paula didn't see them. Maybe they were hiding behind the boxes where we found the body. The killer saw Paula looking around and pulled on the gloves they just happened to have with them before grabbing the knife off the table and killed Paula so quickly she never even screamed."

"Jane Warton is a nurse," Finn pointed out. "She might have gloves on her if she came directly from work, and she would have the know-how to make the first stab fatal."

"Yeah, but we talked to Jane. She said she was in the ladies' room and then went out to the main room and talked to Gwen. Gwen confirmed that she spoke to Jane and several people have confirmed that Jane was in the ladies' room. I don't think it could have been her."

"As long as we're taking about suspects who else have you spoken to and eliminated?"

"So far, we've established alibis for Jane, Barbara, Martha, Alice, and Gwen. We spoke to Giselle, who told us she was outside having a smoke when the whole thing went down. No one remembers seeing her inside the building during the break, but they don't remember seeing her go in or out either. We also spoke to Sarah. She was with Gwen early on, but then she told her she was going to the ladies' room, though no one remembers seeing her after that. We still need to speak to Rachael and Stephanie. We have an appointment with Rachael this afternoon."

"Okay; keep me posted. It looks like the crime scene guys might finish up today. They went back this morning to check a few additional things but seemed pretty confident they'd learned everything they could from the store. I won't know for sure when they'll release the bookstore until later this afternoon. I'll call you when I do."

"Okay; thanks, Finn. And let me know if you track down the owner of the cell. It could be the key to everything."

"All right, and be careful. I don't have a good feeling about this."

I hung up and filled Tara in.

"It doesn't make sense that the killer's prints aren't on the knife," she said.

"Yeah, that definitely adds to the mystery. Let's try to finish the interviews today and then we can go over the suspect list to see if we can narrow it down to one or two people. Once we do that I guess we'll focus on proving our theory."

"Okay. I need to wash my hands and then we can head to the bank to see Rachael. I never did get hold of Stephanie; I'll try calling her again too."

✶✶✶✶✶✶

The Madrona Island Community Bank wasn't a large bank, but it did a steady business and seemed to employ solid, long-term employees who, more often than not, remembered your name. I knew Rachael had worked there for at least ten years, making her way from part-time teller to account manager. She seemed to enjoy her job and based on what I knew of her, she understood the importance of what she did and took it seriously.

"Thank you for meeting with us," Tara said. "I know you're busy."

"I'd like to help, but I only have a twenty-minute break, so we'll need to talk quickly."

I explained that we were talking with everyone who'd been at book club to pick their brains to put together a map of where everyone had been and who they'd spoken to once the break was called. I assured her that we didn't necessarily consider her a suspect but that we hoped she could tell us something that would help us make sense of what had happened.

"When the break was called I went into the coffee bar with everyone else. I poured myself a cup of coffee and helped myself to one of Tara's delicious cookies. Martha was getting some coffee as well and we chatted for a while about the book. At some point Barbara and Alice joined us. I wanted to use the ladies' room before we reconvened, so I excused myself and headed in that direction. I ran into Stephanie, who was just coming out of the ladies' room and we spoke for a few minutes. During that time Sarah showed up and went into the ladies' room. When she came out she and Stephanie went to the coffee bar and I popped into the ladies' room. When I came out I was going to rejoin the others, but the lights went out and you asked everyone to come into the cat lounge. I guess you know the rest."

"You said you ran into Stephanie coming out of the ladies' room when you got there and stopped to chat. Was there anyone else either in the hallway or nearby?" Tara asked.

"Just Sarah, who, as I said, went in before I finished speaking with Stephanie. Other than Sarah and Stephanie, I didn't see anyone. The door to the office was closed and I heard voices inside, though it could have just been Paula talking on the phone."

"One of the others mentioned that you had an argument with Paula in the alley behind the bank not long ago," I began.

Rachael paused with a look of surprise on her face. I supposed her altercation with Paula wasn't widely known. "It was two weeks ago, when she was temping here. There are very definite rules about who can access accounts and for what reason. I found Paula checking accounts for her own information. I don't know what she was after, but when I discovered what she was doing I fired her immediately. She was angry and so was I, and we argued."

"You seemed to be getting along all right at book club," Tara pointed out.

"I wouldn't say we were getting along, but neither of us wanted to make a scene, so we just sort of ignored each other. I know she was upset about being fired, but she had no reason to be looking at the accounts. It was totally inappropriate."

"So, as an account manager you had the authority to fire her?" Tara asked.

"Well, no. It was more that I recommended to bank management that she be let go immediately and they agreed. I spoke to Stephanie after the incident and she told me that Paula had been snooping around in client files when she temped for the law firm she works for too. If you ask me, Paula was after some sort of specific information. Stephanie and I had planned to compare notes to see if the files she accessed at the law firm and the bank belonged to the same people, but we hadn't found the time to get together to do it. I guess now it doesn't matter."

"Not necessarily. It could be important information. Do you think you could provide us with the names associated with the account Paula was snooping around in?"

"If Finn wants that information he can ask for it in an official capacity. You understand; I need to cover my butt. I imagine Stephanie will tell you the same thing."

"You're right. That would be more appropriate and I'll do that." I took the piece of paper I'd torn from Paula's notebook out of my pocket. "Can you at least tell me if these are account numbers associated with this bank?"

Rachael looked at the list and frowned. "The numbers in the first column look like our account numbers. I can't tell you if these specific accounts are in any way associated with the dollar amounts."

"And the last column—are those customer numbers?"

Rachael shook her head. "No. We don't have customer numbers that look like that. I'm not sure what those are. They don't look familiar."

I folded the paper and put it back in my pocket. "Is there anything else you can tell us about Paula or anything that happened the night she died?"

"No, not really. I will say after working with Paula for almost two weeks I saw she wasn't the sweetheart she seemed to be in book club. In fact, I'd say she was carrying around a lot of suppressed rage. If she hadn't been the victim I'd have suspected her of being the killer. That woman seemed to be battling a lot of demons, I can tell you that."

"Did she ever mention anyone she was having a specific problem with?" I asked.

"Other than her poor, long-suffering husband, not really."

"Do you know Henry?"

"Actually, I do. He works for Calvin and Coleman, a local accounting firm."

"Is that the same firm Paula temped for?"

"No. She temped for Brian Walton. He has a one-man office. The firm Henry works for has three accountants and a bookkeeper."

"Okay. Go on. You were saying you know Henry from his work with this firm."

"Yes. We've met to discuss client issues on several occasions and we took a class together in Portland last summer. And no, we aren't now nor have we ever been involved in a sexual relationship. In fact, Henry seemed to be totally loyal to Paula. We had a drink when we were in Portland last summer and he said he wanted to get home early because Paula was having a hard time. He told me she'd had a tragic past and had hired a PI to look into something for her, but the PI wasn't coming through the way she'd hoped and it was causing her a lot of stress."

"Do you know who the PI was or what he was looking for?" I asked.

Rachael shook her head. "Henry never said. I'm not even sure he knew, but I suppose you can ask him."

"Yeah. I will. Does the name Amber mean anything to you?"

"In relation to Paula, no. I know a young woman named Amber who lives on the island, but I don't have any reason to believe she and Paula were acquainted. Still, if you want to follow up with her, her last name is Fox and she lives in Harthaven. She works for the little general store down by the marina. She just moved to the island last summer after graduating high school, so it's doubtful she knew Paula, but I guess it couldn't hurt to ask."

"Yeah, I will. Is there anything else you can tell me?"

Rachael paused and then continued. "There is something, although I have no idea if it means anything. Henry mentioned that the reason he and Paula moved to Madrona Island three years ago was because she'd been sick and he hoped a change of scenery would help her recover. Now, he never specified what it was she was sick with, but I kind of got the idea based on his tone of voice and the way he chose his words that he was referring to a mental ailment rather than a physical one. I might be way off, but if you're really trying to learn everything you can about her, you might want to check with Henry."

"I will," I repeated.

"You also might want to speak to Jane Warton. She was closer to Paula than the others at book club. If Paula was having a problem of some sort she might have confided in Jane."

"We've already talked to Jane, but that was a good suggestion. During her time working as a temp at the bank did Paula have the ability to withdraw funds or move money?" I suddenly asked.

"You're thinking the dollar amounts next to the account numbers represent money Paula may have stolen? The answer is no. Paula was able to receive deposits and cash checks written for an amount not to exceed two hundred dollars, but she wasn't in a position to withdraw or move the kind of money on the paper you have. I'm not sure why she wanted the information she did, but it was completely inappropriate and my gut tells me that while she couldn't withdraw the funds, she was interested in something specific."

"Would she have been able to pull up account balances?"

"Yes, she could have watched accounts even if she couldn't withdraw money from them."

"Okay, that's helpful. I know you're busy, so thank you for taking the time to speak to us."

Tara and I returned to her car. I could see a storm brewing on the horizon and hoped we would be able to complete our interviews before it hit. Tara turned on the heater while we sat in her car discussing what to do. We both thought it was a good idea to have Finn ask about the names on the accounts Paula was accused of accessing, so I called him while Tara tried to reach Stephanie once more. It was important to speak with her as soon as possible. It seemed the fifth time was a charm because Stephanie not only answered her cell but she told us she was off that day and we were welcome to swing by her house. She lived in Harthaven near the marina, so we decided to see if Amber Fox was at work and then head on over to Stephanie's.

Chapter 11

Amber was a tall, thin eighteen-year-old with thick blond hair she allowed to curl down her back. She had dark brown eyes, fair skin, and a smattering of freckles across her nose. When she smiled her entire face lit up, seeming to welcome you to come in to the store and sit a spell.

"Hi, y'all. How can I help you?"

"Are you Amber?" I asked.

"Yes, ma'am, I am."

"I'm Cait and this is my friend, Tara. We're talking to people about our friend Paula today and wondered if you knew her."

"The lady with the heart necklace?"

"Heart necklace?"

Amber pulled a necklace out from under her blouse. "I met a woman a few months ago named Paula. She told me she

147

had a necklace just like mine and wondered where I'd gotten it. I told her my mama gave it to me and we got to talking. She seemed nice and I'm new to the island, so I don't really know anyone and was happy for the company. A few days later she came in and asked me if I wanted to go to dinner with her. I was surprised she asked because I'm a lot younger than her, but, like I said, I was lonely and she was nice, so I agreed to go."

"And how'd it go?" Tara asked.

"Fine at first. But then, toward the end of the meal, she asked me if I'd been adopted. I told her I wasn't. She asked if I was sure, which I thought was kind of a strange question to ask, but I went ahead and told her I popped out of mama's belly at the Piggly Wiggly in front of a whole lotta witnesses, so I was pretty sure. After that she changed the subject."

Amber took a deep breath before she went on. "Then, maybe a few weeks later, she came in again and asked where I grew up. I told her Georgia. She asked when my birthday was and I asked her why she wanted to know. She said she was just curious and didn't mean to be inappropriate. She told me she knew someone who looked a lot like me who was born on April 12, 1999. I remembered that she'd asked about my being adopted and almost didn't answer, but she seemed harmless and really sad, so I told her I was born in February. I figured if she had it in her head that I was somehow this person she knew, my being born in a different month should prove she had the wrong person. She thanked me and left."

"Did you see her again after that?" I asked.

"No, ma'am. My boss told me she came in last week looking for me, but I was off and he wouldn't tell her where I lived."

"Okay, well, thank you for your time. It's been nice talking to you."

"Are you related to Danny Hart?" the girl asked as I turned to leave. "You have the same eyes."

"Danny's my brother."

The girl lowered her gaze. "Do you know if he has a girl?"

"I think maybe he does."

I wasn't sure whether Danny was currently in a relationship or not, but if Amber was looking at his eyes she was interested in more than just a simple friendship with a guy who I knew would chew her up and spit her out.

"I wonder if the tragedy in Paula's life had to do with someone named Amber,"

Tara mused. "The birthdate Paula gave Amber was the first one on the paper."

"I realized that as soon as she mentioned it. Joy mentioned the second date was right around the time Paula moved here."

"Maybe something happened to Amber. Maybe she was kidnapped or something, and this Amber not only has the same necklace but she's about the same age and maybe looks like her."

We got into the car.

"I wonder if Henry knows who Amber is," Tara said.

"I don't suppose it would hurt to ask him. Let's go see Stephanie and then regroup," I suggested.

"Why don't you call Finn first?" Tara suggested. "He should be able to get Paula's medical records. Maybe Amber was Paula's daughter. I know she never mentioned having children, but maybe she did have a daughter and something happened to her. Maybe seeing this Amber resulted in her depression cycle starting up again."

"I'm not sure that's how depression works, but I would be interested in finding out about the girl Paula spoke to Amber about. I'll call while you drive."

I got hold of Finn, who shared that the crime scene team had already requested Paula's medical records and confirmed she'd delivered a child, a daughter, on April 12, 1999, in Mobile, Alabama. Finn said he didn't know what had become of the child, and when he'd asked Henry about it, he said he had no idea Paula had ever given birth. Henry told Finn he'd met Paula during the summer of 2002 in Colorado and she didn't have a child with her at that time. Paula had never mentioned the name Amber to him. All I could do was assume Paula had given her baby up for adoption and, based on my assumption that Amber Fox would be about the same age as Paula's baby, I further concluded that the baby Paula had given away had been named Amber as well.

******

Stephanie Abrams had been a legal secretary for Brown and Bidwell, a law firm that served not only Madrona but nearby islands as well, for two years and was working on getting licensed as a paralegal.

"Thank you for seeing us," Tara said. "We know you're busy, so we'll try to be quick."

"I appreciate that. I do have a busy day. How can I help you?"

I offered the usual explanation that we were attempting to map the movements of the book club members after the break that night, and asked Stephanie who she spoke to and who she remembered seeing.

"When the break was first called I headed to the ladies' room. There were several people waiting, so I got in line behind Alice."

"Alice told us Paula entered the office just as she was coming out of the ladies' room. Do you remember Paula going into the office just as you were going in to the ladies' room?"

"Yes, I do. She seemed to have something on her mind and I didn't speak to her, but I did see her. When I came out of the bathroom I saw Rachael coming in my direction and I stopped to chat with her."

"How long would you say you spoke to Rachael?" I asked.

"Maybe five minutes."

"Did anyone else go into the ladies' room while you were in the hallway?"

"Sarah. She showed up shortly after I began talking with Rachael."

"And did you see Sarah come out of the ladies' room?"

"Yes. She came out just as I was wrapping up my conversation with Rachael. She wanted to speak to Paula, but she was still on the phone in the office, so we walked back to the coffee bar together. I lost track of her when the lights went out."

"Did Rachael stay behind after you left?"

"I think she may have ducked into the ladies' room."

"Do you remember seeing Giselle at all during that time?"

"I saw her going out first thing after the meeting broke up. I think she wanted to grab a smoke. I didn't see her come back in, but she was there when we all huddled together in the cat lounge. I know that for a fact because I could smell the smoke."

Tara made a few notes while I formulated my next question. After a moment I said, "We found a notebook Paula used to keep lists, phone numbers, appointments, that sort of thing. There was one page in particular that caught our eye." I pulled the list with the three columns out of my pocket. "Rachael verified that the first column has account numbers for the bank she works for. She said the third column didn't have anything to do with the numbering system at the bank. She also said you caught Paula going through confidential files when she worked for Brown and Bidwell. Is it possible the third column of numbers is for client numbers for this firm?"

Stephanie looked at it and frowned. "Yes. These are client numbers."

"Would you be willing to share with us which clients the numbers are associated with?"

"Not without a warrant."

"Rachael mentioned you planned to compare notes to see whether Paula was looking at the client and bank numbers of the same people. Did you ever do that?"

Stephanie shook her head. "Not yet, but given this new information, I think we should."

"Do you have any idea why Paula wanted this information?" I asked.

"Off the top of my head I'd say she was either blackmailing someone or had plans to do so. I can't tell you who the account numbers belong to any more than Rachael could share who the bank account numbers refer to, but if I were you and I wanted to know what Paula was up to, I'd have your brother-in-law get a warrant for information relating to the numbers from both the bank and this firm."

"I'll do that."

We spoke to Stephanie for a while longer and then thanked her for her time and left. I looked up at the dark clouds that had intensified while we were inside the firm. It looked like the rain would find its way onshore any minute. I hoped the storm wouldn't be as intense as Tuesday's storm, but after the long hot summer we'd had rain would be welcome.

"So now that we've talked to everyone, do you have a feel for who our main suspect is?" Tara asked after we'd returned to her car and were heading to my cabin.

"Not really. Let's go through the notebook again. We only skimmed the first quarter of it. Maybe there's a clue hidden in the rest of it somewhere."

"We should follow up with Finn on the accounts."

"Yeah, we should. I'll call him when we get to the cabin. He should know by now when the crime scene guys are going to release the bookstore as well. If they let it go today do we even want to open tomorrow? I feel like we need time to clean up a bit."

"Yeah, I thought of that too. Let's plan to reopen on Tuesday either way. Maybe we'll have the murder solved by then. I think I'll feel better about being in the building if we can find justice for Paula and put the matter to rest."

******

At the cabin, I called Finn, who informed me that he was working on a warrant; then I poured glasses of iced tea for Tara and me and we settled around my small kitchen table with the notebook and a pen and paper for taking notes. I wanted to get things straight in my mind. It seemed like we didn't have any suspects, but I knew we had to be missing something, so we decided to go over the statements of all the women again. I got out the white board we'd begun to refer to as a murder board and began to record the details of our conversations.

"Okay," Tara began, "Jane told us that after we called for the break she went directly to the ladies' room. When she came out Barbara, Alice, and Stephanie were in line. That's been confirmed by all of them, so as far as I'm concerned all four have alibis for the beginning of the break."

"We know, based on what both Alice and Stephanie have said, that Paula went into the office to make her call as Alice was coming out of the ladies' room and Stephanie was going in," I added. "That means it's the placement of the women after that point that's the most important because so far no one has admitted to seeing Paula after she was in the office. You know what's odd…" I stopped to really think things through. "Alice said she saw Paula enter the office as she was coming out of the ladies' room. Stephanie, who was just going in, confirmed it. Not one person has reported seeing Paula before she entered the office, but we know at least several minutes passed between the time we called for the break and Paula asked to use the phone. I wonder where she was during that time."

"Good question, although I don't suppose it really matters. We know Paula was alive when she went into the office just as Alice was coming out of the ladies' room and Stephanie was going in. We know Jane was speaking to Gwen and Martha was speaking to Barbara. We also know Alice joined them at that point, so let's cross Martha, Jane, Gwen, Barbara, and Alice off our suspect list and focus more closely on Giselle, Sarah, Stephanie, and Rachael."

Tara glanced at the notes she'd been taking. "Giselle said she was outside smoking when all of this was going on. No one actually saw her during that time, though Stephanie did say she saw her leave the building and she smelled like smoke when she came back. Still, there's no way to know if Giselle could have snuck back in after having a cigarette and killed Paula before we got back together in the cat lounge, so I think we have to assume Giselle doesn't have an alibi and leave her on the suspect list."

"Agreed. What about Sarah?" I asked. "We know she was speaking to Gwen early in the break, although Gwen told us that when Sarah saw Paula head for the office she followed her. Sarah said that when she was outside the office she heard Paula on the phone and decided to use the ladies' room, which was empty. When she came out Paula was still on the phone, so she went to the coffee bar with Stephanie, who had been speaking to Rachael. Stephanie said much the same thing."

"So it sounds like Sarah and Stephanie have alibis as well," Tara said. "According to Stephanie, Rachael stayed behind when she and Sarah went to the coffee bar.

Rachael said she popped into the ladies' room and when she came out she was about to rejoin the others, but the lights went out. It seems the only two we don't have firm alibis for at the time we estimate Paula must have died are Giselle and Rachael."

"Okay; let's take a closer look at them. Jane and Barbara both told us Paula believed Henry was having an affair with Giselle. Giselle denies that, as does Henry, but that doesn't mean they aren't lying or that Giselle didn't kill Paula. She could easily have had time to have a cigarette, which would account for the smoky smell Stephanie mentioned, snuck back in, killed Paula, and eventually gone back to the group."

"I think we need to dig into Giselle and the rumor of her affair with Henry. It does seem like she might have motive for wanting Paula out of the way. As for Rachael, we know she and Paula had an altercation when Paula was temping at the bank. Rachael said Paula was looking through files she wasn't allowed to look at, and Paula did have a list in her notebook that appears to be related to bank accounts. I think we need to try to figure out what Paula was up to and how it might involve Rachael as well."

"Okay; where should we start?" I asked.

"We really didn't go through the notebook all that carefully. Let's look at it page by page to see if anything else pops up."

I refilled the iced tea glasses while Tara began slowly and methodically looking through the notebook. Most of the pages held information that seemed to have little if any value. We had the page with the three columns and Rachael had confirmed that the first column was account numbers, although she wouldn't tell us who they belonged to or why Paula might have them. The second column contained dollar amounts that at this point I assumed related to the bank accounts. And the third column were customer numbers associated with the law firm.

We'd also found the phone number associated with the call Paula had made just before she died, though so far Finn hadn't had any luck tracking what it belonged to.

Most of the pages in the notebook did contain items like appointment reminders and shopping lists. There was one appointment that stood out because it was circled and highlighted: *Colin—Tuesday 10/24*. October twenty-fourth was the day

Paula had died, so I wondered if this Colin was either involved in her death or at least had an idea of what had been on her mind. Of course, a first name wasn't much to go on, although it wouldn't hurt to ask Jane, Barbara, Joy, and even Henry if the name meant anything to them.

Toward the back of the notebook, Tara found the most interesting thing of all: a small key taped to an otherwise blank page. I had no idea what it opened, but it looked like the kind that would open a locker or safety deposit box, so I removed it from the page and safely secured it on a chain I put around my neck. I figured I wouldn't lose it that way, and if I happened to figure out what it opened I'd have it with me and wouldn't have to come back home to get it.

"Even if we do find out what the key goes to, and we discover what Paula was doing with the bank account and client numbers, there are still only a finite number of people who had the opportunity to kill Paula," Tara pointed out. "We've narrowed it down to Rachael or Giselle. Both seem to potentially have motive. It seems to me the only way for us to prove either of them did it is to find physical evidence putting them in the storage room."

"Do you specifically remember seeing either woman after the lights went out?"

"I saw them both as they left."

"Were they wearing jackets?"

Tara looked at me. "You're back to the blood spatter anomaly."

"I think it has to be considered. If you're standing close enough to a person to stick a knife into their heart you're going to get blood on you. There's no way around it."

"I guess that's a weak spot in our theory that one of the women from book club killed Paula," Tara admitted. "I do remember seeing Rachael and Giselle as they were leaving and they did have their coats on. I suppose the coat the killer was wearing was hiding the blood, but it still seems likely they'd have it on their skin. Sure, they could have washed up, but it still seems something would have alerted us that something was going on."

"The lights were out and it was dark. We could ask some of the others if they specifically remembered seeing Rachael and Giselle after the electricity failed, but I agree we're going to need something concrete if we want to solve this case."

Chapter 12

Friday, October 27

Finn called me the next morning with the news that the bookstore would be released from restrictions by noon. I told him we'd decided to clean up but not reopen until Tuesday. Cody was coming home later this afternoon and I also wanted to clean the cabin and wash my hair.

I asked Finn about the warrant for the bank and law client account numbers. He informed me that the judge hadn't felt they had a good enough reason to fulfill such a request. I wasn't certain the information on the notepaper was relevant to the case and decided it might not hurt to speak to both Stephanie and Rachael one more time.

I called Tara and we made plans to meet at Coffee Cat Books at noon. In the meantime, I went to the closet for the cleaning supplies I would need to turn my messy cabin into a romantic getaway. I was just about to head into the kitchen to give it a good scrub when Frank ran to the door and began scratching to get out.

I paused and looked at him. "You have a cat box," I reminded him.

He continued to scratch, so I opened the door. Frank trotted directly out to my car and began to scratch at that door as well.

"You want to go somewhere?"

"Meow."

"Now really isn't a good time. I need to clean up the place, shower, and meet Tara at noon."

"Meow," Frank insisted.

I took a deep breath and let it out slowly. "Okay. If you're sure it's important. Let me get my keys. Do you have a way of letting me know where you want me to go?"

Frank just looked at me.

"Okay, how about this: I'll ask you questions and if the answer is yes, you meow. If the answer is no, you stay quiet. Will that work?"

"Meow."

"Fantastic. Does our destination have to do with Paula's murder?"

Frank remained quiet.

"Okay, then does the destination have to do with Paula in any way?"

"Meow."

"So you want to show me something that relates to Paula but doesn't necessarily have anything to do with her murder?"

"Meow."

"Do you want me to drive to her house?"

Silence.

"Is it related to the account numbers we found?"

"Meow."

"Do you want me to go to the bank?"

Silence.

"The law office where she temped?"

Silence.

"Okay; I can figure this out. You want to show me something relating to the account numbers, but you don't want me to go to her house, the bank, or the law office. How about whatever it is the key opens?"

Silence.

"Her car?"

"Meow."

"Okay, great. You want me to take you to her car. Now I just need to figure out where her car ended up."

I went inside to call Finn again. He told me the car was at the impound lot for the time being. I asked if Frank and I could look at it and he said he'd meet us there. I begged him to give me twenty minutes, then ran in, took a quick shower, slipped into clean clothes, and headed to the lot.

Finn was waiting when we arrived. I opened the door so Frank could hop out and he trotted directly to the car and pawed at the door. Finn opened it and Frank jumped in onto the backseat and began pawing at something under the driver's seat. Finn reached in and pulled out a small diary. Inside was handwriting I assumed was Paula's. On the first page was the name Andy Wong. After that name was a number I'd learned was associated with one of the Brown and Bidwell customer numbers. Beside that was one of the bank account numbers and next to it was a note that said, *involuntary manslaughter, 2013*.

On the following page was the name Cindy Gardner. After it was a customer number, followed by a bank account number and the words, *embezzlement, 2015.*

I looked up at Finn. "What if Paula was snooping around and came across client information connecting to people she knew lived in this area? Maybe the information she found was sensitive, so she used it in some sort of blackmail scheme? That would explain the bank account numbers and the dollar amounts."

"So you think she was killed by someone she was blackmailing?"

I looked through the rest of the diary. There were six names in all, none of them related to anyone in book club. "I'm not sure. None of the names are of anyone in the book club. The only way one of these people could have killed Paula is if they were, as Sarah suggested, already hiding in the building when the book club members arrived or they were working with someone in the club who let them in the side door. Both are possible, but neither seems likely. Still, it wouldn't hurt to speak to these people to see if anything pops."

"I'll take care of that this morning and let you know what I find."

"Great. In the meantime, I need to head over to Coffee Cat Books to help Tara with the cleanup. I'll have my cell with me, so call me as soon as you know something."

I decided to take Frank to the bookstore with me. There was no reason to drive all the way home just to drop him off. I figured we'd only be at the store for two or three hours and I could take him home when we were finished there.

"Wow," Tara said after I'd filled her in. "You really think Paula was blackmailing people?"

"It looks that way, but right now all we have are random pieces of data that seem to fit but may not. I know Cindy Gardner and I don't remember her ever being arrested or going to jail. The note said *embezzlement, 2015*. That was just two years ago, so if something like that played out in the courts I would have remembered. My guess is, if she was guilty of embezzlement her attorney might have worked something out that would keep her out of jail and her name out of the news. If Paula came across it and threatened to expose what she'd done to her friends and neighbors, I could see how she might be persuaded to pay her off to protect her secret."

"Okay, say that's true; why would Paula do it?"

I shrugged. "Maybe she needed the money."

Tara looked less than convinced.

"Rachael and Joy both said she'd hired a PI. Maybe she needed the money to pay him."

"I guess that's as good an explanation as any. It'll be interesting to see what Finn finds out. In the meantime, I think we should tackle the storeroom first. Finn sent someone over to clean up the blood and remove the yellow flags and chalk marks, but the boxes are still shoved back against the wall. I think we should reorganize so we can find the merchandise we need when we reopen on Tuesday."

"Okay. I'm glad Finn took care of the blood."

"Me too. I was kind of freaked out by the idea of having to deal with it."

Tara and I worked side by side for over an hour while Frank watched from the sidelines. The boxes were heavy and moving them back to where they'd originally been stored was a dirty and exhausting chore. I was about to move a box from the last stack needing to be relocated when Frank darted across the room and pounced on something that had been under the last box on the pile.

"What did you find?" I asked Frank, who was batting at the object.

I bent over and picked it up. I held it up so Tara could see it. "It's an earring," I said. "Do you remember if anyone from book club was missing an earring?"

"I didn't notice, but we can ask around. If it belongs to one of the book club women it places her at the crime scene. This could turn out to be an important clue. The crime scene guys must have stacked the boxes on top of it without even seeing it."

"I'll take a photo of it and send it to Finn. If we can match the earring to the owner we really might have something."

Tara and I finished up in the storage room, then headed to the main part of the building, where the coffee bar and bookstore were. It didn't take us long to dispose of the trash that had been left from Tuesday's refreshments. Once the room was tidied, I vacuumed and dusted everything while Tara restocked both the coffee bar and the bookshelves. We were just finishing up when Finn called.

"Well?" I asked after answering my cell.

"You were right. Paula was blackmailing all six people named in the diary. Each of the victims had done something illegal and, in most cases, embarrassing and career ending. In all six instances one of the attorneys at Brown and Bidwell had worked out a plea deal that kept them out of jail and out of the news. Paula must have found the files while she temped there. That part isn't totally clear."

"How long had this been going on?" I asked.

"Just a couple of months. She asked each of her blackmail victims for a single payment. I was able to obtain a warrant to look at Paula's bank records. It appears all the money was put into one account and the only withdrawals from it were made in the name of Walton Smith. I'm trying to track him down."

"That's great. Maybe he has the rest of the puzzle. Did you get the photo of the earring?"

"I did. It matches the one that was found on Paula's left lobe when she was brought into the morgue. I'm assuming she dropped the other earring at some point."

Well, that was a bummer. An earring belonging to the killer would have been a lot more useful.

I spoke with Finn for a few more minutes before hanging up, then filled Tara in as we finished up and prepared to leave for the day.

"Are you going home after this?" I asked as heavy rain began to fall. It looked like we might be in for another hard storm.

"I'm having dinner with Sister Mary. We've been trying to get together once a week just to talk."

I knew how badly Sister Mary wanted Tara to be comfortable with everything she'd learned so recently but decided not to mention the conversation I'd had with her on Wednesday. "That's nice. Are you enjoying your time together?"

Tara nodded. "It's really helping me to get to know her as a person. I've always liked and admired her, but now I'm finding I'm beginning to have feelings for her beyond that of a respected role model. She's been really great about helping me work though the fact that she's my mother." Tara was quiet for a moment and then said, "Actually, accepting and embracing the idea that Sister Mary is my mother is less strange for me than the idea that Jane and Jim Farmington were my parents. It's hard dealing with the trauma my mother must have endured at the hands of my father, who was a very cruel man."

"It is a tragic story," I agreed. "But it seems as if Sister Mary is in a good place.

She's happy with the life she ended up with."

"She is. I asked her once if she ever thought about all that money she left behind when she ceased to be Maryellen Thornton, and she said she wouldn't trade the life she has now for all the money in the world. She's been through so much and she seems to have found a way to find peace with her situation. I know it's up to me to do the same."

I hugged Tara. "You're an amazing woman. You know I'm always here for you."

"I know. And that means a lot. I'm glad I have you to talk to about this. I don't think I'd be able to handle it if I were in it alone. I do, however, find it difficult to keep such a big secret from everyone other than the very small handful of people who know. I can't even tell Parker, which feels wrong to me. I hate to lie to him, but on nights like tonight, when he asks me out on the same night I have plans with Sister Mary, I have to lie and say I have a headache or prefer to stay in."

"Why lie? Sister Mary is a nun you've known and been close to for most of your life. It wouldn't be weird at all for you to have made dinner plans with her even if she wasn't your mother."

Tara sighed. "I'm overthinking this, aren't I? I do that sometimes. I make things a lot more complicated than they have to be."

"I think you have a very good reason to be a bit off-balance, but yeah, I think you are overthinking things. The next time you plan to meet Sister Mary just be honest with Parker. If he thinks it's odd—and I don't think he will—just remind him that you've attended St. Patrick's your whole life and have developed a relationship with her. And eventually, if things progress with Parker, I'm sure Sister Mary will support you if you decide you want to tell him the truth."

Tara smiled a tired little smile. "I know you're right. Have a wonderful reunion with Cody tonight."

I grinned. "Don't worry; I plan to."

Chapter 13

By the time Cody got home the rain had begun to clear. He wanted to check in with Mr. Parsons and then suggested we grab a bite in town before coming back to my place for the night. I knew Cody worried about Mr. Parsons when he was away, but I'd checked in with him often, as had his good friends Francine Rivers and Banjo and Summer Reynolds.

When we arrived at Mr. Parsons's house he was watching an old movie with Francine so we didn't stay long, but Cody did notice the supplies in the refrigerator were getting low, so we decided to stop by the grocery while we were out and bring back the items we purchased before heading back to my cabin.

"So, tell me about the murder you've been working on," Cody said after we'd ordered pizza and beer at the new pub in Pelican Bay.

"We started out with nine suspects because we knew early on that the killer had to have been one of the women at the book club meeting. We've eliminated all but two of them: Giselle Bowman and Rachael Steinway. To be honest, even though we haven't verified alibis for them, my gut tells me that they didn't do it. The problem is, if we do eliminate Giselle and Rachael we're down to zero suspects."

"And you're sure the other seven women are all in the clear?" Cody asked after taking a sip of his beer.

"Pretty sure. We asked the women about their movements between the time we took a break and the time the lights went out and we all gathered in the cat lounge. Those seven women all reported either speaking to someone or seeing others speaking to others during that time. Tara and I created a timeline, and it looks like these women were all accounted for. Giselle said she went outside to smoke. Unfortunately, no one other than Stephanie saw her leave and no one saw her come back in at all. She was around later, but she had time to go out, smoke a cigarette, sneak back in, kill Paula, and then rejoin the group."

"How easy would it have been for her to come in and make her way to the storeroom without being seen?"

"It would have been nearly impossible for most of the evening, but once the lights went out and the storm intensified, anyone could have snuck in and killed Paula. The women were all gathered in the cat lounge by that point and the thunder was so intense that even if Paula had called out we most likely wouldn't have heard her."

"Did Giselle have a motive for killing Paula?"

"It seems she might have. According to several of the women, Paula told them Giselle was sleeping with her husband. Giselle denied it, but that doesn't mean it wasn't true. On the other hand, all the women who knew Paula told us she'd been acting oddly and, over the course of the past few weeks, changed her story about Henry's affair."

Cody folded his hands on the table. "Okay, so based on what you've told me, it sounds like Giselle had both probable motive and means. Tell me about Rachael."

"Rachael's movements were verified with the others until the very end. She'd been chatting with Martha and then excused herself to go to the ladies' room. Stephanie was just coming out when she got there, so she stopped to chat with her for a minute. Meanwhile, Sarah showed up and went into the ladies' room. When Sarah came out she rejoined the main group with Stephanie while Rachael stayed behind. No one remembers seeing her after that point until the very end of the evening, when everyone was leaving. In other words, no one remembers her coming back from the ladies' room, which is in the same hallway as the office. It could be that she met Paula in the hallway or even went into the office and confronted her. I'm not sure how or why they ended up in the storeroom, but it does seem like a possibility."

"Did Rachael have motive?" Cody asked.

"Yes, she did. It turns out that during the time she was temping for Brown and Bidwell, the law firm Stephanie works for, Paula searched customer files that seem to have provided her with sensitive information she used to blackmail six people. Once she had the blackmail information she temped at the bank, where Rachael found her checking bank account records she wasn't authorized to access. Rachael had Paula fired and they had a verbal altercation in the alley behind the bank. I image both Stephanie and Rachael felt used and betrayed that Paula would come into the businesses they worked for, steal sensitive information, and use if for her own purposes."

Cody took another sip of his beer before he asked his next question. "Do you know if she was successful in getting money from those six people?"

"Finn verified that she received a onetime payment from them. She had the money transferred to someone named Walton Smith. Finn is trying to track him down, but my intuition tells me that he'll turn out to be the PI several of the women mentioned Paula had hired."

"Do we know why she hired a PI?"

I shrugged. "Originally, I felt it was to prove her husband was cheating, but now I'm not so sure. Paula asked to use the office phone on the night of the storm because hers was dead. We determined she called a number leading to a burner cell Finn hadn't been able to track down as of the last time I spoke to him. I have a feeling it could be the private investigator's. We found a note Paula jotted down while seated at the desk: Amber and the dates April 12, 1999, and November 6, 2014. We also know Paula had spoken to a teenager named Amber who works in the general store by the Harthaven Marina. She asked the girl, who happened to be eighteen and also happened to have a necklace similar to one Paula told her she owned, if she was adopted. The girl told her she wasn't. Finn later found out that Paula had given birth to a female child on April 12, 1999. That made me wonder if Paula hadn't hired the PI to find Amber. If that's so, I think we'll find Walton Smith is the owner of the burner cell Paula called and the recipient of the money she got from her blackmail victims."

We stopped speaking as the pizza was delivered. Cody topped off both our beers from the pitcher we'd ordered before resuming the conversation. I took a bite of the delicious pie, chewing slowly to enjoy the blend of tomato, pepperoni, and olives.

"Okay; let's summarize. You feel it was one of the book club members who killed Paula and the only two without firm alibis are Giselle and Rachael."

I nodded.

"You also believe Paula may have hired a PI to find a child she gave birth to in 1999. It seems possible she blackmailed six people to pay the PI, although none of the victims are considered suspects in her death because they weren't in the bookstore building on the night Paula died."

"Correct."

"Do you have any other clues?"

"I found a key taped to the inside of a notebook we found in Paula's home. I don't know what it unlocks, but it looks like the sort of thing that might go to a safety deposit box, a locker, or some other small lock."

Cody ate in silence for a few minutes. I could tell by the look on his face that he was concentrating on the information I'd just provided. God, I'd missed him while he was away.

"I take it the crime scene guys didn't find any fingerprints in the storeroom that might have belonged to the killer?"

I shook my head. "They found mine and Tara's, as well as yours, Danny's, and the three part-time workers' we had over the summer. They even found Paula's, but not a single print from any other book club member. Paula's were also the only prints found on the murder weapon other than mine and Tara's. Finn is pretty sure the killer wore gloves. It appears no attempt was made to wipe prints off anything."

"So unless your book club members carry around gloves the murder must have been premeditated."

"It would seem so," I agreed. "It was a stormy night, but not nearly cold enough to warrant hats and mittens. Jane's a nurse, so we considered she might have had gloves on her if she'd just come from work, but she has an alibi for the entire evening. I can't think of a reason for anyone else to have had gloves in their possession. I also don't see how it could have been premeditated. Sure, the killer might have suspected Paula would be at the meeting, but they couldn't have known the storm would be strong enough to have us take a break, or that Paula would ask to use the phone, providing a situation where she was isolated from the rest of the group. We have to be missing something."

"I agree it doesn't add up." Cody frowned as he appeared to be thinking some more. "Let's talk about the key you found. Do you have it with you?"

"Yes."

"Have you tried to find the lock it goes to? Maybe that's what you need to pull this together."

"Not really. I wouldn't even know where to start."

"What about Paula's house? Maybe the key goes to a lockbox."

"I guess that would be the easiest place to start. I know a way in through the cellar."

"Okay. Let's head over there after we eat to see what we can find. If we don't find the lock there we'll make a list of other possibilities."

"Do you want to grab the groceries you want to buy for Mr. Parsons first? The market is going to close in an hour and I'm not sure how long it will take to look for the lock."

"Yeah. We'll head to the market, drop everything off, then head over to Paula's house."

******

Madrona Island had several small minimarts that sold snacks and drinks but only one grocery store. It was crowded on Friday night, as islanders stocked up for the weekend. Cody didn't have a list, but he seemed to know what he wanted to buy, so I followed behind him as he loaded up a cart with fresh produce, lean cuts of meat, and a few dairy products. I knew Mr. Parsons had a sweet tooth, so I suggested getting a treat as well. We had just entered the bakery aisle when a petite woman with long brown hair and bright blue eyes let out a little screech and came running toward me.

"Caitlin Hart." The woman hugged me hard. "It's been ages since I've seen you."

"Oh my God, Noel." I hugged my old friend in return before taking a step back and getting a better look at the woman I'd known in my childhood. "Are you on the island visiting your aunt?"

"Actually, I'm moving back, at least temporarily." Noel glanced at Cody with a question in her eyes.

"Cody West, this is Noel Wasserman," I introduced. "Noel and I were friends all through grade and middle school, but I haven't seen her since she moved the summer before high school."

Noel and Cody exchanged nods and then Cody suggested I catch up with her while he finished his shopping. I was thrilled to see my old friend and agreed to his plan.

"So where did you find the hunk?" Noel's eyes danced with amusement as Cody walked away.

"Cody went to the same school we did growing up, but he was two years ahead of us. He was friends with my brother Danny."

Noel frowned and then her eyes grew big. "Oh wait, I remember him." She glanced in the direction Cody had taken. "He certainly has filled out nicely. I seem to remember he was as skinny as a rail when he was young."

"Yeah, I guess he was. So what have you been up to?"

Noel's smile faded, as did her cheerful demeanor. "In a nutshell, graduating high school, going to college, becoming an agent for the FBI, getting married, becoming a widow, and coming back to the island."

"A widow? Oh no. What happened?"

"My husband was also an agent for the FBI. He was killed in the line of duty eight months ago. I tried to return to the life we'd built together, but I had a hard time dealing with things, so I decided to come back to the place I've always considered home."

I took Noel's hand in mine and gave it a squeeze. "I'm so very sorry to hear about your husband. I can't imagine how difficult this must be."

"Thank you. It's been hard since Brad died, but I think I'm beginning to get some perspective. Being back on the island is really helping and my aunt has been great."

"Do you still work for the FBI?" I asked.

Noel tucked a lock of her long dark hair behind her ear. "No. I never really planned to join the FBI. When I first attended college I took a bunch of math and technology classes. I really wasn't all that focused on my endgame, but I love to tinker with computers and I love to travel and I'm fluent in five languages. I guess I thought I'd figure out a way to combine all that into a fantastic global career. And then I met Brad during my sophomore year. Brad was an agent for the FBI and convinced me that my background in math, technology, and languages would make me a valuable asset. I wasn't sure I even wanted to go get involved, but Brad and I continued to hang out and eventually, I realized I was in love with him. Brad introduced me to some people and, long story short, I dropped out of school and signed on as an analyst. The work was interesting, but after Brad died I found myself getting restless, so I quit and took my aunt up on her offer to stay with her for a while. I honestly have no idea what I want to do at this point, but she's convinced me to take my time and find my passion, so that's exactly what I'm doing."

"Wow. That's some story." I looked across the store. "It looks like Cody is about done, but I'd love to meet for lunch or even coffee next week."

"I'd love it too. What's your cell number? I'll text you my contact information and we'll plan a time to really catch up. By the way, my name is Noel Christmas now."

I paused before I reacted. "Noel Christmas? Are you pulling my leg?"

"I wish I was. Brad's last name was Christmas. When he asked me to marry him I insisted on keeping my maiden name, but then at the last minute I realized that I wanted to share his name, so I changed it."

I smiled. "Well, I love it and I think it fits you. I'll call you and we'll definitely get together next week."

By the time I said good-bye to Noel, Cody was in line at the checkout stand, where I joined him. I was glad to see he'd picked up a couple of treats. Cody took his role as Mr. Parsons's friend seriously and made sure the elderly gentleman had plenty of healthy food to eat. He kept an eye on the amount of sugar he ate, which at times became a sore spot between them.

"So, how's your friend?" Cody asked.

"She's good, except for the fact that she was recently widowed."

"I'm sorry to hear that."

"Yeah. I bet it's rough. We're going to get together for lunch next week. Did you remember Mr. Parsons's cereal?"

"No. I forgot it."

"I'll run and grab it. I know he's out because he mentioned it to me when I went to see him earlier in the week."

I turned and headed down the cereal aisle. I was standing on tiptoe to reach the top shelf when a hand reached over my shoulder and grabbed the box I was aiming for. I turned to see Rachael holding the box.

"This what you wanted?" she asked.

"Yes. Thanks. Height does have its advantages."

Rachael handed me the box. "I spoke to Finn. I guess he told you about the whole blackmail thing."

"Yes, he did."

"I have to say, when he told me what was going on I was furious. To think Paula would treat her neighbors that way."

I took a breath and let it out. "Yeah. I was surprised too. I imagine she must really have needed the money, but the way she went about getting it wasn't cool at all."

"I feel like she used Stephanie and me. We both recommended her when she showed interest in the temp assignments. Now I not only feel like a fool, but I feel partially responsible for what happened to those people. I know Stephanie feels even worse."

I looked back to the front of the store. There were still two people in front of Cody. "It wasn't your fault, or Stephanie's either. Paula was a friend of sorts and you were trying to help her out by giving her a recommendation. There's no way you could have known what she planned to do. Paula was obviously a troubled woman who was struggling with demons none of us knew about. I don't approve of what she did, but I'm beginning to understand how she could have done it."

"I guess that's true, although it doesn't make me feel any better. Oh, did you speak to Jane?"

"Not since I spoke to you."

"She found a photo on her phone she didn't even know she'd taken. She got out her phone to use as a flashlight when the power went out and somehow ended up taking a photo. Anyway, if you look closely you can see everyone, except for you and Tara, who were in the cat lounge, Paula, me, because I was still making my way back from the ladies' room, and of course Jane, who was the one taking the photo. I figured it might help you with the map you were trying to create."

"Thanks. I am interested. I'll call Jane and have her text the photo to me."

I joined Cody in line with the cereal just as he reached the front. I told him I needed to make a call and headed to the very front of the store. Jane was on her way out the door but promised to forward the photo to me when she got to work.

"Something going on?" Cody asked after he joined me.

"Maybe. I ran into Rachael, who informed me that Jane has a photo she took by accident of everyone at the bookstore just after the power went out. She's going to forward it to me. I'll get to see where everyone was standing at that critical point in time."

Jane sent the photo just as we arrived at Mr. Parsons's house. I sat at the kitchen table and studied it while Cody put the groceries away. The first thing I noticed was Giselle coming in the front door. If she'd gone out to smoke and stayed outside until the power went off, there was no way she could have killed Paula. Martha, Alice, and Barbara were all standing near one another, Stephanie was talking to Sarah, and Gwen was standing closest to the photographer, who I already knew was Jane, which just left Rachael. I didn't see her in the photo, but she had said she was still making her way back from the ladies' room. The photo didn't clear her, though it would be odd for her to tell me about it if she thought it would implicate her. I was beginning to think Paula's killer really wasn't one of the book club members, but if not one of them, who?

Once Cody had finished we returned to his truck and headed to Paula's house. I hoped we'd find something there because I was clean out of ideas.

"This whole thing makes no sense," I complained. "I feel like I've eliminated every single book club member, but Paula is dead and if one of them didn't do it, who did?"

"Maybe Paula killed herself," Cody suggested.

I frowned. "She was stabbed. How could she have killed herself?"

"You said the knife entered her body from a spot just below the sternum and was thrust in at an upward motion toward the heart. Think about it: If you had a good grip on the knife and drove it in hard enough and at the right angle, you could totally stab yourself in the heart."

I thought about it and supposed Cody had a point. It would be possible. "But why? I mean, even if she was depressed and wanted to end it all why would she use such a brutal method and why would she do it at book club and not in the privacy of her own home?"

"You said she made a phone call. Maybe whatever news she received was enough to set her off."

I couldn't imagine that anyone would receive news bad enough that would make them stab themselves in the heart, which was a brutal and, I was sure, painful way to go, but the knife did have Paula's prints on it, and no one else's other than Tara's and mine, and she had been suffering from a bout of depression that may have ended up getting the best of her.

"How can we prove it if that's what happened?"

"I don't know. Maybe it can be proven forensically or maybe we can figure out a strong enough motive for Paula to have done it."

"I should call Finn," I said.

"Yeah, that might be a good idea."

Finn was on the other line when I called, but he promised me he'd call me right back. Cody and I let ourselves into Paula's house and began to look around.

We'd decided to start in her bedroom. It seemed the most logical place to keep something she valued enough to lock up. After about fifteen minutes Cody found a metal box with a small lock. I tried the key and it opened to reveal the clothes and toys of a child. There was also a birth certificate showing that Paula Kline had given birth on April 12, 1999, to a baby named Amber Kline, as well as a handful of photos of Paula holding a young child of about two or three. The line on the birth certificate where the father's name should have been listed was blank.

My phone rang just as we'd come across a journal. I handed it to Cody to answer it.

"Hey, Finn. Thanks for calling me back. We have a new theory." I explained about the suicide angle.

"I think you might be on to something," Finn replied. "Someone finally picked up when I dialed the number for the burner cell. As we suspected, the phone belongs to Walton Smith, and he was the private investigator Paula hired."

"Why did she hire him?"

"To find the daughter she gave birth to in 1999. It took him months to track her down because no formal adoption ever occurred, but after weeks of diligent searching he found the answers he was looking for."

Suddenly, everything was falling into place. "She died, didn't she?"

"Worse. She was murdered."

I took a deep breath and put my hand over my mouth. Poor Paula. She must have received the news while alone in the office.

Finn continued when I didn't speak. "According to Mr. Smith, Paula became pregnant while living on the streets. She had no idea who the baby's father was and she suffered from mental health issues and drug addiction. She could barely take care of herself, little alone a baby."

"So she gave her up for adoption," I realized.

"She sold her."

"What?" I screeched.

"She needed a fix and she didn't have any money, so some guy she knew who dealt in all sorts of illegal activity offered to buy Amber, who was three by this time, for five thousand dollars. Paula was desperate and agreed to the sale and never saw Amber again. She did wonder what had become of her, though. Then she saw Amber from the store by the marina, and not only was she the right age, but she had similar coloring to her

Amber and a locket that looked exactly like one she'd given to her daughter the last time she was with her. She was certain the Amber from the store was her daughter even though she said she wasn't adopted. Paula realized she needed proof, so she hired Smith to prove this Amber was her daughter. She thought it was fate intervening to give her a second chance."

"But it wasn't her?"

"No, it wasn't. Smith eventually picked up the trail of Paula's Amber. She wound up with a couple in a black-market transaction, so the adoption papers were forged, though they looked authentic enough that no one ever questioned them. Amber's new father was physically abusive, so she ran away when she was only fourteen. A year later, on November 6, 2014, her body was found under an overpass near Atlanta, Georgia. The cause of death was strangulation."

"Oh God." I felt like I was going to throw up.

Cody must have noticed that I'd gone totally white because he set down the journal and gathered me into his arms, then took the phone from my hands, which were shaking.

"It's Cody. Cait's pretty shaken up."

He listened to what Finn had to say and eventually said, "Okay. Thanks, Finn.

"He's going to have the medical examiner look at Paula's body again to see if the suicide idea fits. He thinks it will. I'm so sorry, Cait." Cody gathered me into his arms as I sobbed for both Amber and Paula and all the lives that had been so needlessly wasted.

Chapter 14

Saturday, October 28

Siobhan showed up at my cabin the next morning just as I was getting ready to head over to the haunted house. Cody had spent the night with me but had left early to spend some time with Mr. Parsons before he needed to show up in town for the Halloween festivities.

"Are you okay?" Siobhan asked after entering my side door and hugging me in an offer of comfort.

"Yeah. What happened to Paula's daughter was tragic, and I can't imagine how Paula must have felt when she found out, but I think I have some perspective now. If nothing else, I guess I understand Paula's depression and even her paranoia.

It must have been hard to live your whole life knowing you'd sold your daughter for a fix, never knowing how her life turned out."

"I can't imagine."

I squeezed Siobhan's hand. "Cody and I had a long talk last night and he made me see that, while I can mourn the senseless loss of two lives, the burden of their deaths isn't mine to bear. I feel like I have a new outlook this morning and am pretty much determined to embrace the day. Are you going to the haunted house?"

She shook her head. "Finn and I have other plans. I did want to share some news with you before you head out for the day, though."

My smile faded. "I hope it's not bad news."

"Not unless you consider being an aunt for the first time bad news."

"You're having a baby?"

"I'm having a baby," Siobhan confirmed as I hugged her a bit more tightly than one should probably hug a pregnant woman.

"When?" I asked as I placed my hand on Siobhan's flat stomach.

"My due date is June fifth."

"Do you know if it's going to be a boy or a girl?"

"Not yet."

"Oh my God, Siobhan." I hugged her again. "You must be so happy."

"I am. And Finn is too."

"Does Mom know?"

"Not yet. I'm going to tell her, Cassie, Aiden, Danny, and Maggie today. Finn told me about Paula and her baby and I figured you could use some good news to brighten your day, so I headed here first."

"Thank you." I hugged Siobhan a final time. "You really have put some sunshine in my day."

We chatted for a while longer and then I headed over to the haunted house. I was looking forward to volunteering today. Having a fun community event to focus on would help me forget the tragedy I very much wanted to relegate to the back of my mind. As promised, the haunted house was spookier than it had been in years, which suited my mood perfectly. Cody showed up about twenty minutes after I did dressed as a zombie I couldn't resist wanting to kiss.

"You'll get makeup all over your face." Cody laughed when I kissed him over and over again.

"I don't care. I missed you."

"I've only been gone for two hours."

"Which, if you ask me, is two hours too long. Did you have a nice visit with Mr. Parsons?"

"I did. I think it meant a lot to him that I took the time to sit with him for a while before coming into town. It seems Francine, Summer, and Banjo did a good job of ensuring he wasn't alone much when I was away."

"Someone was there every time I stopped by," I verified. "Tara and Parker invited us to join them for a late dinner tonight. Are you up for that?"

"Sounds good." Cody used his thumb to wipe away some of the makeup that had smeared from his face to mine. "I'm glad to see your sunny smile is back."

"It's hard to be depressed when you find out you're about to be an aunt for the first time."

"Finn and Siobhan?"

I nodded. "Isn't that exciting? I can't wait!"

"That *is* exciting and you're going to make a wonderful aunt." Cody looked toward the door to the back room, where the staging was taking place. "I need to go, but I think we're done about the same time, so wait for me by the front door and I'll meet you as soon as I change and wipe this goo off my face."

"Okay. I kind of like the zombie look, but I don't suppose it would be appropriate to wear to dinner."

Cody chuckled. "I don't suppose so, but maybe we can arrange a private showing at some point."

I just grinned as he kissed my nose and walked away.

My job this year was to sell tickets at the booth, so that was where I headed. It would have been fun to dress up and be part of the cast, but it was also nice to have the opportunity to chat with friends and neighbors as they arrived. I work in a business that provides me with the chance to visit with other islanders on a regular basis, but there were still those who didn't read or drink coffee I rarely came into contact with.

"Tara, Sister Mary," I greeted the mother-daughter pair. "Are you here to put some fright in your Halloween?"

"We are." Tara nodded. "Sister Mary and I are going to the kiddie carnival with Parker and Amy as soon as he gets off work, but in the meantime, we thought we'd see what all the hoopla is about."

"I haven't been through yet, but those who have say it's pretty awesome." I couldn't help but notice that not only were both women grinning but they were holding hands. Seeing Tara so happy after everything she'd been through did my heart good. "Are we still on for dinner tonight?"

"If we can meet at around eight. Sister Mary is going to sit with Amy for a couple of hours after we finish up at the carnival and the church festivities."

"Eight is good. Antonio's?"

"Sounds perfect."

The line grew long after Tara and Sister Mary left, so I didn't have the opportunity to say much more than hi to those who showed up during peak time. I was at the point where I needed a bathroom break when Amber from the marina general store stepped up at the window.

"Amber, hi," I greeted her. "Are you here to check out the haunted house?"

"I was walking by and saw you standing here. Can we talk for a minute?"

"Sure. Just let me get someone to cover for me."

It took a few minutes, but eventually, I found another volunteer to watch the window while I took a break. "What can I do for you?" I asked.

"I lied the other day when you were by. I'm not sure why, but I've been thinking about it, and when I saw you standing here I knew I needed to say something about it."

"Okay. Let's sit down over here." I led her to a small seating area. "What do you want to tell me?"

"When Paula came in and started asking questions she seemed sort of desperate. It kind of freaked me out, so when she asked about the necklace I said my mom had given it to me, but that wasn't true. I met a girl, also named Amber, who was my same age and lived on the street when I was visiting my aunt in Atlanta four years ago. She needed money and I gave her what I had, which was a couple hundred dollars I'd been saving up for my trip. I knew she might be scamming me, but she was so young. It scared me that she seemed to be in a position where she was taking care of herself, and she said her name was Amber like mine. I guess I just wanted to help. She started to cry when I gave her everything I had. She said it was too much, but I insisted. She said she wanted to give me something in return, so she gave me the necklace. When Paula asked about it I wanted to tell her the truth, but I was scared."

"That's totally understandable. Paula was out of line to pursue you so aggressively," I said. Then I added, "It turned out the girl who gave you the necklace was her daughter and she'd been looking for her."

"Oh no. I'm so sorry. I didn't know. Did she find her?"

I shook my head. "It was a long time ago. Even if you had told Paula the truth about the necklace it wouldn't have made a difference." I decided not to mention that Amber was dead. Why burden the poor girl with the knowledge?

"I'm sorry I didn't agree to spend more time with Paula after that first dinner. I feel bad she died without finding her daughter. It's just been so hard for me since my parents died and I moved here. I don't really know anyone, and sometimes I feel vulnerable and alone. I know it just takes time to get settled, but it's so hard to go home to an empty apartment every day. I hear all these sounds and I'm afraid my mind makes more out of them than it should. I've been having nightmares and I feel myself being suspicious of everyone and everything. Maybe I should get a dog."

I was about to respond when Frank trotted in and headed right for us. "What about a cat?" I said as Frank jumped up onto her lap.

"Oh my. Who are you?" Amber said with a smile on her face.

"His name is Frank and he's a totally awesome cat. I think with him by your side all your nightmares will disappear."

I'd learned not to wonder how the cats got out of my cabin and made their way around the island, but I'd realized as soon as he set eyes on Amber that she'd found someone to help her through this difficult time.

******

"This is nice," I said to Cody much later that evening. We'd had an awesome day and a wonderful dinner with Parker and Tara and had just spent the last hour making up for all the nights we'd missed in each other's arms.

"It is nice." Cody ran a finger up my bare arm as I cuddled next to him with my head on his bare chest. "This last trip was a hard one. I always miss you, but this one was the worst."

"I guess I'll have to come with you next time. I know you're busy during the day, but at least we can be together at night. I hate not seeing you for weeks at a time. I know you're doing a really important thing and I'm proud that you're helping to save lives, but I'll be glad when you're done."

Cody kissed the top of my head. "Yeah. Me too. At least I'll be home through the holidays."

"Which I'm very happy about."

"When I was talking to Mr. Parsons today he asked me about doing a Christmas Eve dinner again this year. I told him I'd talk to you about it. I know it's turned into something that requires a lot of work on both our parts, so I didn't want to tell him we'd do it without discussing it with you."

"I'd love to do it again," I replied. "Granted, our original idea of a small meal with a few friends has turned into a huge social event requiring weeks of planning, but I can see how much it means to Mr. Parsons to have people in the house again. We should start making a list right away so we don't accidentally leave anyone out. I'd like to invite Amber. I had a chat with her today. She told me she's been feeling lonely since moving to the island, so I called Cassie earlier and she's going to go by the general store to introduce herself. They're close enough in age that I'm hoping they'll hit it off."

"It's nice of Cassie to make the effort."

"She seems to have turned into an adult while I wasn't looking. She told me the other day she's planning to go to college and was worried about Mom being alone. I told her I'd make sure she was okay when she was away. I know Mom has Gabe and I think she'll be fine, but I hate to think of anyone being lonely."

Cody flipped me over onto my back, then looked deeply into my eyes as he ran a finger down my cheek and across my jaw. "You know I love you."

My heart began to pound as our souls connected. "I love you too."

"You're such a caring, giving person. You amaze me every day with your open heart and your generosity toward all creatures great and small. I'm so grateful to have you in my life and I can't imagine spending even one day without you by my side. I want to grow old with you, have a family with you, and experience all that life has to offer with you. Caitlin Hart, will you marry me?"

I put my open hand up to Cody's cheek. I wanted to say something touching and memorable, but all I could do was nod as tears streamed down my face. I wrapped my arms around Cody's neck and he lowered his head and gently brushed his lips to mine.

A New Series from
Kathi Daley Books

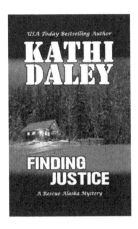

Sample Chapter for
Finding Justice

There are people in the world who insist that life is what you make of it. They'll tell you that if you work hard enough and persevere long enough, everything you've ever desired will one day be yours. But as I sat in the fifth dingy office I'd visited in as many months and listened as the fifth pencil pusher in a dark suit and sensible shoes looked at me with apologetic eyes, I finally understood that not every dream was realized and not every wish granted.

"Ms. Carson, do you understand what I'm saying?"

I nodded, trying to fight back the tears I absolutely would not shed. "You're saying that you can't consider my grant application unless I've secured a facility."

The man let out a long breath that sounded like a wheeze, which I was sure was more of a sigh of relief. "Exactly. I do love your proposal to build an animal shelter in your hometown, but our grant is designed to be used for ongoing operations. I'm afraid without a physical presence we really must move on."

I leaned over to pick up my eight-year-old backpack. "Yes. I understand. Thank you so much for your time."

"Perhaps next year?" the man encouraged with a lopsided grin.

I smiled in return. Granted, it was a weak little smile that did nothing to conceal my feelings of defeat. "Thank you. I'm certain we'll be able to meet your criteria by the next application cycle."

"We begin a new cycle on June 1. If you can secure a facility by that time please feel free to reapply," the man said.

I thanked the bureaucrat and left his office. I tried to ignore the feeling of dread in the pit of my stomach and instead focused on the clickety-clack that sounded as the tile floor came into contact with the two-inch heels I'd bought for this occasion. Had I really been working on this project for more than two years? Maybe it was time to throw in the towel and accept defeat. The idea of building an animal shelter in Rescue Alaska was a noble one, but the mountain of fund-raising and paperwork that needed to be scaled to make this particular dream come true seemed insurmountable at best.

I dug into my backpack for my cell phone, which rang just as I stepped out of the warm building into the bracing cold of the frigid Alaskan winter. I pulled the hood of my heavy parka over my dark hair before wrapping its bulk tightly around my small frame.

"So, how did it go?" My best friend, Chloe Rivers, asked the minute I answered her call.

"It went."

"What happened?" Chloe groaned.

I looked up toward the sky, allowing the snow to land on my face and mask my tears. "The grant is designated for operations, so it seems we aren't eligible until we have a facility. The problem is, we have no money to build a facility and no one will give us a loan for one unless we have capital for operations already lined up. It's an endless cycle I'm afraid we can't conquer."

"We can't give up. You know what you have to do."

"No," I said firmly. "We'll find another way." I knew I sounded harsh, but I had to make Chloe understand.

"Another way?" Chloe screeched. I listened as she took a deep breath before continuing in a softer tone. "Come on, Harmony, you know we've tried everything. There *is* no other way."

Chloe's plea faded as an image flashed into my mind. I closed my eyes and focused on the image before I spoke. I knew from previous experience that it was important to get a lock on the psychic connection before I said or did anything to break the spell. Once I felt I was ready, I opened my eyes and tuned back into Chloe's chatter. I was certain she hadn't missed a beat even though I'd missed the whole thing. "Look, I have to go," I interrupted. "Someone's in trouble. I'll call you later."

I hung up with Chloe, called a cab, and then called Dani Mathews. Dani was a helicopter pilot and one of the members of the search-and-rescue team I was a part of. She'd offered to give me a lift into Anchorage for my meeting today and I'd taken her up on it.

"Someone's in trouble," I said as soon as Dani answered.

"I was about to call you. I just got off the phone with Jake." Jake Cartwright was my boss, brother-in-law, and the leader of the search-and-rescue team. "There are two boys, one fifteen and the other sixteen. They'd been cross-country skiing at the foot of Cougar Mountain. Jake said they have a GPS lock on a phone belonging to one of the teens, so he isn't anticipating a problem with the rescue."

The cab pulled up and I slipped inside. I instructed the driver to head to the airport, then answered Dani. "The boys dropped the phone, so Jake and the others are heading in the wrong direction"

I slipped off my shoes as the cab sped away.

"Do you know where they are?" Dani asked with a sound of panic in her voice.

"In a cave." I closed my eyes and tried to focus on the image in my head. "The cave's shallow, but they're protected from the storm." I took off my heavy parka and pulled a pair of jeans out of my backpack. I cradled the phone to my ear with my shoulder as I slipped the jeans onto my bare legs.

"Where's the cave, Harm?"

I closed my eyes once again and let the image come to me. "I'd say they're about a quarter of a mile up the mountain."

"Are they okay?" Dani asked.

I took a deep breath and focused my energy. There were times I wanted to run from the images and feelings that threatened to overwhelm and destroy me, but I knew embracing the pain and fear was my destiny as well as my burden. "They're both scared, but only one of them is hurt. Call Jake and tell him to check the cave where we found Sitka," I said, referring to our search-and-rescue dog, who Jake and I had found lost on the mountain when he was just a puppy. "And send someone for Moose." I glanced out the window. The snow was getting heavier, and it wouldn't be long before we would be forbidden from taking off. "I'm almost at the airport. Go ahead and warm up the bird. I should be there in two minutes."

I hung up the phone and placed it on the seat next to me. The driver swerved as I pulled my dress over my head and tossed it to one side. I knew the pervert was watching, but I didn't have time to care as I pulled a thermal shirt out of my backpack, over my head, and across my bare chest.

"What's the ETA to the airport?" I demanded from the backseat.

"Less than a minute."

"Go on around to the entrance for private planes. I have the code to get in the gate. My friend is waiting with a helicopter."

As the cab neared the entrance, I pulled on heavy wool socks and tennis shoes. I wished I had my snow boots with me, but the tennis shoes would have to do because the boots were too heavy to carry around all day.

As soon as the cab stopped, I grabbed my phone, tossed some cash onto the front seat, and hopped out, leaving my dress and new heels behind.

"You've forgotten your dress, miss."

"Keep it," I said as I flung my backpack over my shoulder and took off at a full run for the helicopter. As soon as I got in, Dani took off. "Did you get hold of Jake?" I asked as I strapped myself in.

"I spoke to Sarge. He's manning the radio. He promised to keep trying to get through to Jake. The storm is intensifying at a steady rate. We need to find them."

"Moose?"

"Sarge sent someone for him."

I looked out the window as we flew toward rescue. A feeling of dread settled in the pit of my stomach. The storm was getting stronger and I knew that when a storm blew in without much notice it caught everyone off guard, and the likelihood of a successful rescue decreased dramatically.

The team I belonged to was one of the best anywhere, our survival record unmatched. Still, I'd learned at an early age that when you're battling Mother Nature, even the best teams occasionally came out on the losing end. I picked up the team radio Dani had tucked into the console of her helicopter, pressed the handle, and hoped it would connect me to someone at the command post.

"Go for Sarge," answered the retired army officer who now worked for Neverland, the bar Jake owned.

"Sarge, it's Harmony. Dani and I are on our way, but we won't get there in time to make a difference. I need you to get a message to Jake."

"The reception is sketchy, but don't you worry your pretty head; Sarge will find a way."

"The boys are beginning to panic. I can feel their absolute horror as the storm strengthens. The one who isn't injured is seriously thinking of leaving his friend and going for help. If he does neither of them will make it. Jake needs to get there and he needs to get there fast."

"Don't worry. I'll find a way to let Jake know. Can you communicate with the boys?"

I paused and closed my eyes. I tried to connect but wasn't getting through. "I'm trying, but so far I just have a one-way line. Is Jordan there?" Jordan Fairchild was not only a member of the team but she was also a doctor who worked for the local hospital.

"She was on duty at the hospital, but she's on her way."

"Tell her she'll need to treat hypothermia." I paused and closed my eyes once again. My instinct was to block the pain and horror I knew I needed to channel. "And anemia. The break to the femur of the injured teen is severe. He's been bleeding for a while." I used the back of my hand to wipe away the steady stream of tears that were streaking down my face. God, it hurt. The pain. The fear. "I'm honestly not sure he'll make it. I can feel his strength fading, but we have to try."

"Okay, Harm, I'll tell her."

"Is Moose there?"

"He will be by the time you get here."

I put down the radio and tried to slow my pounding heart. I wasn't sure why I'd been cursed with the ability to connect psychically with those who were injured or dying. It isn't that I could feel the pain of everyone who was suffering; it seemed only to be those we were meant to help who found their way into my radar. I wasn't entirely sure where the ability came from, but I knew when I'd acquired it.

I grew up in a warm and caring family, with two parents and a sister who loved me. When I was thirteen my parents died in an auto accident a week before Christmas. My sister Val, who had just turned nineteen, had dropped out of college, returned to Rescue Alaska, and taken over as my legal guardian. I remember feeling scared and so very alone. I retreated into my mind, cutting ties to most people except for Val, who became my only anchor to the world. When I was fifteen Val married local bar owner Jake Cartwright. Jake loved Val and treated me like a sister, and after a period of adjustment, we became a family and I began to emerge from my shell. When I was seventeen Val went out on a rescue. She got lost in a storm, and although the team had tried to find her, they'd come up with nothing but dead ends. I remember sitting at the command post praying harder than I ever had before. I wanted so much to have the chance to tell Val how much I loved her. She'd sacrificed so much for me and I wasn't sure she knew how much it meant to me.

Things hadn't looked good, even though the entire team had searched around the clock. I could hear them whispering that the odds of finding her alive were decreasing with each hour. I remember wanting to give my life for hers, and suddenly, there she was, in my head. I could feel her pain, but I also knew the prayer in her heart. I knew she was dying, but I could feel her love for me and I could feel her fighting to live. I could also feel the life draining from her body with each minute that passed.

I tried to tell the others that I knew where she was, but they thought they were only the ramblings of an emotionally distraught teenager dealing with the fallout of shock and despair. When the team eventually found Val's body exactly where and how I'd told them they would, they began to believe that I really had made a connection with the only family I'd had left in the world.

Of course, the experience of knowing your sister was dying, of feeling her physical and emotional pain as well has her fear as she passed into the next life, was more than a seventeen-year-old could really process. I'm afraid I went just a bit off the deep end. Jake, who had taken over as my guardian, had tried to help me, as did everyone else in my life at the time, but there was no comfort in the world that would undo the horror I'd experienced.

And then I met Moose. Moose is a large Maine Coon who wandered into the bar Jake owned and I worked and lived in at the time. The minute I picked up the cantankerous cat and held him to my heart, the trauma I'd been experiencing somehow melted away. I won't go so far as to say that Moose has magical powers—at least not any more than I do—but channeling people in life-and-death situations is more draining than I can tolerate, and the only one who can keep me grounded is a fuzzy Coon with a cranky disposition.

"Are you okay?" Dani asked as she glanced at me out of the corner of her eye. Her concern for my mental health was evident on her face.

"I'm okay. I'm trying to connect with the boys, but they're too terrified to let me in. It's so hard to feel their pain when you can't offer comfort."

"Can't you shut if off? I can't imagine allowing myself to actually feel and experience what those boys are."

"If I block it I'll lose them. I have to hang on. Maybe I can get through to one of them. They don't have long."

"Do you really think you have the ability to do that? To establish a two-way communication?"

I put my hand over my heart. It felt like it was breaking. "I think so. I hope so. The elderly man who was buried in the avalanche last spring told me that he knew he was in his final moments and all he could feel was terror. Then I connected and he felt at peace. It was that peace that allowed him to slow his breathing. Jordan said the only reason he was still alive when we found him was because he'd managed to conserve his oxygen."

"That's amazing."

I shrugged. I supposed I did feel good about that rescue, but I'd been involved in rescues, such as Val's, in which the victim I connected with didn't make it. I don't know why it's my lot to experience death over and over again, but it seems to be my calling, so I try to embrace it so I'm available for the victims I can save like that old man.

"The injured one is almost gone," I whispered. "They need to get to him now."

I knew tears were streaming down my fact as I gripped the seat next to me. The pain was excruciating, but needed to hang on.

Dani reached over and grabbed my hand. "We're almost there. I'm preparing to land. Sarge is waiting with Moose."

She guided the helicopter to the ground despite the storm raging around us. As soon as she landed, I opened the door, hopped out, and ran to the car, where Sarge was waiting with Moose. I pulled him into my arms and wept into his thick fur. Several minutes later I felt a sense of calm wash over me. I couldn't know for certain, but I felt as if the boy I was channeling had experienced that same calm. I looked at Sarge. "He's gone."

"I'm so sorry, Harm."

"The other one is still alive. He's on the verge of panicking and running out into the storm. Jake and the others have to get to him."

Sarge helped me into the car and we headed toward Neverland, where I knew the fate of the second boy would be revealed before the night came to an end.

Recipes

Double Layer Pumpkin Pie—submitted by Darla Taylor
Pumpkin Cinnamon Pancakes—submitted by Vivian Shane
Marie's Gingersnaps—submitted by Marie Rice
Streusel Apple Pie—submitted by Patty Liu

Double Layer Pumpkin Pie

Submitted by Darla Taylor

8 oz. cream cheese, softened
1 tbs. milk
1 tbs. sugar
1 tub (8 oz. or larger) Cool Whip
1 prepared graham cracker crust
1 cup cold milk
1 can (16 oz.) pumpkin
2 pkgs. (4 serving size) vanilla instant pudding
1 tsp. ground cinnamon*
½ tsp. ground ginger*
¼ tsp. ground cloves*

May substitute 1 slightly heaping tsp. pumpkin pie spice for the * items above.

Mix cream cheese, 1 tbs. milk, and sugar in large bowl with wire whisk until smooth. Gently fold in 1½ cups Cool Whip. Spread onto bottom of crust.

Pour 1 cup cold milk into large bowl. Add pumpkin, pudding mixes, and spices. Beat with wire whisk until well mixed. Mixture will be thick. Spread over cream cheese layer.

Refrigerate at least 4 hours. Garnish with remaining Cool Whip.

Pumpkin Cinnamon Pancakes

Submitted by Vivian Shane

The first pumpkin recipe I make when the fall season arrives.

Pecan syrup:
1 cup maple-flavor syrup
5 tbs. chopped pecans, toasted

Pancakes:
1 cup buttermilk pancake mix
⅔ cup cold water
⅓ cup canned pumpkin
½ tsp. cinnamon
⅛ tsp. ginger
Butter, room temperature

Combine syrup and pecans and heat in microwave on high, about 25 seconds. Set aside and keep warm.

In a medium bowl, whisk pancake mix, water, pumpkin, cinnamon, and ginger until just blended (don't overmix; the batter will be lumpy). Spray griddle with baking spray and heat to 350 degrees (medium). Spoon 2 tbs. batter onto griddle for each pancake. Cook for 2 minutes or until bubbles appear, then turn over and cook 2 minutes longer. Top with butter and syrup.

Yields 6 pancakes

Note: I use the leftover pumpkin for pumpkin bread.

Marie's Gingersnaps

Submitted by Marie Rice

¾ cup shortening
1 cup brown sugar
¼ cup molasses
1 egg
2¼ cups all-purpose flour
2 tsp. baking soda
1 tsp. ground ginger
1 tsp. ground cinnamon
½ tsp. ground cloves

Preheat oven to 350 degrees.

In a large bowl, cream together the first four ingredients until fluffy. In a separate bowl, sift the remaining ingredients together. Stir the flour mixture into the molasses mixture.

Lightly spray baking sheets. Form dough into small balls and roll in granulated sugar. Place 2 inches apart on the sheets. Bake for about 10 minutes or until the desired firmness/hardness. (For crunchier cookies, leave in oven longer.)

Cool for a couple of minutes on baking sheet and then move cookies to cooling rack to finish cooling. If reusing the baking sheet for another batch, use spatula to scrap the sheet and then respray before placing more cookie dough on the sheet.

Makes about 5 dozen cookies.

Streusel Apple Pie

Submitted by Patty Liu

1 Pillsbury Pie Crust, unbaked
½ cup granulated sugar
2 tbs. flour
¾ tsp. cinnamon
¼ tsp. nutmeg
¼ tsp. salt
6 cups apples, sliced

Topping:
1 cup uncooked quick or old-fashioned oats
⅓ cup brown sugar, firmly packed
⅓ cup pecans, finely chopped
½ tsp. cinnamon
⅓ cup butter or margarine, melted

Preheat oven to 350 degrees. Combine filling ingredients, except apples; toss apples in mixture; place in 9-inch pie shell. Combine topping ingredients; spread over pie filling. Bake 50 minutes or until topping is brown and apples are tender.

Serves 8

Note: You can microwave the apples until softer; this will cut down on the baking time. Remember, if you use apples with peel it will take longer. Doubling the topping gives better coverage for this pie. It's important to cover the edges of the pie crust with tin foil *before* baking to keep the crust from getting too brown.

Books by Kathi Daley

Come for the murder, stay for the romance.

Zoe Donovan Cozy Mystery:
Halloween Hijinks
The Trouble With Turkeys
Christmas Crazy
Cupid's Curse
Big Bunny Bump-off
Beach Blanket Barbie
Maui Madness
Derby Divas
Haunted Hamlet
Turkeys, Tuxes, and Tabbies
Christmas Cozy
Alaskan Alliance
Matrimony Meltdown
Soul Surrender
Heavenly Honeymoon
Hopscotch Homicide
Ghostly Graveyard
Santa Sleuth
Shamrock Shenanigans
Kitten Kaboodle
Costume Catastrophe
Candy Cane Caper
Holiday Hangover
Easter Escapade
Camp Carter
Trick or Treason – *September 2017*
Reindeer Roundup – *December 2017*

Zimmerman Academy The New Normal
Ashton Falls Cozy Cookbook

Tj Jensen Paradise Lake Mysteries by Henery Press:
Pumpkins in Paradise
Snowmen in Paradise
Bikinis in Paradise
Christmas in Paradise
Puppies in Paradise
Halloween in Paradise
Treasure in Paradise
Fireworks in Paradise – *October 2017*
Beaches in Paradise – *June 2018*

Whales and Tails Cozy Mystery:
Romeow and Juliet
The Mad Catter
Grimm's Furry Tail
Much Ado About Felines
Legend of Tabby Hollow
Cat of Christmas Past
A Tale of Two Tabbies
The Great Catsby
Count Catula
The Cat of Christmas Present
A Winter's Tail
The Taming of the Tabby
Frankencat
The Cat of Christmas Future – *November 2017*
The Cat of New Orleans – *February 2018*

Seacliff High Mystery:
The Secret
The Curse
The Relic
The Conspiracy
The Grudge
The Shadow
The Haunting – *September 2017*

Sand and Sea Hawaiian Mystery:
Murder at Dolphin Bay
Murder at Sunrise Beach
Murder at the Witching Hour
Murder at Christmas
Murder at Turtle Cove
Murder at Water's Edge
Murder at Midnight – *October 2017*

Writers' Retreat Southern Seashore Mystery:
First Case
Second Look
Third Strike
Fourth Victim – *October 2017*
Fifth Night – *January 2018*

Rescue Alaska Paranormal Mystery:
Finding Justice – *November 2017*

A Tess and Tilly Mystery:
The Christmas Letter – *December 2017*

Road to Christmas Romance:
Road to Christmas Past

Kathi Daley lives with her husband, kids, grandkids, and Bernese mountain dogs in beautiful Lake Tahoe. When she isn't writing, she likes to read (preferably at the beach or by the fire), cook (preferably something with chocolate or cheese), and garden (planting and planning, not weeding). She also enjoys spending time on the water when she's not hiking, biking, or snowshoeing the miles of desolate trails surrounding her home.

Kathi uses the mountain setting in which she lives, along with the animals (wild and domestic) that share her home, as inspiration for her cozy mysteries.

Kathi is a top 100 mystery writer for Amazon and won the 2014 award for both Best Cozy Mystery Author and Best Cozy Mystery Series.

She currently writes six series: Zoe Donovan Cozy Mysteries, Whales and Tails Island Mysteries, Sand and Sea Hawaiian Mysteries, Tj Jensen Paradise Lake Mysteries, Writers' Retreat Southern Mysteries, and Seacliff High Teen Mysteries.

Giveaway:

I do a giveaway for books, swag, and gift cards every week in my newsletter, *The Daley Weekly*
http://eepurl.com/NRPDf

Other links to check out:
Kathi Daley Blog – publishes each Friday
http://kathidaleyblog.com

Webpage – **www.kathidaley.com**

Facebook at Kathi Daley Books – **www.facebook.com/kathidaleybooks**

Kathi Daley Teen – **www.facebook.com/kathidaleyteen**

Kathi Daley Books Group Page – **https://www.facebook.com/groups/569578823146850/**

E-mail – **kathidaley@kathidaley.com**

Goodreads – **https://www.goodreads.com/author/show/7278377.Kathi_Daley**

Twitter at Kathi Daley@kathidaley – **https://twitter.com/kathidaley**

Amazon Author Page – **https://www.amazon.com/author/kathidaley**

BookBub – **https://www.bookbub.com/authors/kathi-daley**

Pinterest – **http://www.pinterest.com/kathidaley/**

Made in the USA
Middletown, DE
13 September 2020